POLLY's
SMALL TOWN WAR

J.E. Christer

Published in 2008 by YouWriteOn.com

First Edition

Published by YouWriteOn.com

Dedicated to the Memory of My Father.
A gentleman in every sense of the word.

And with Love and Grateful Thanks
To My Mother whose wartime memories
made this story possible.

Chapter 1

Barton upon Humber - 1935

"Wake up you idle eejit and get some work done around here."
Polly's awakening was abrupt as she felt someone shaking her
roughly. She opened her eyes to find her brother-in-law pushing his
unshaven face close to hers. She recoiled from the stench of his
breath, and pulled the threadbare blanket up instinctively under her
chin. She responded with as much hatred as she could throw into her
sleepy voice.

"Get your filthy face out of mine, Sean O'Connell and leave me
alone," she kept her voice low to emphasise every word. He drew
back his hand to slap her but she was too quick for him and scrambled
past him to stand in the middle of the kitchen with her hands on her
hips, her thin nightgown offering little protection against the cold
morning. Sean, selfish as always, had banished her from her cosy
bedroom upstairs to a make-shift bed in the kitchen. Polly's sister,
Laura, walked in and took in the scene before her, judging correctly
that Sean had instigated yet another argument. She sat down heavily
on a kitchen stool and dragged her lank hair back from her face.

"What's going on here then?" she asked almost with reluctance, the
tiredness in her voice plain for Polly to hear.

"I've told her to get some work done around here - all she ever does
is lie in that pit of hers," Sean swung round to see Polly standing
behind Laura, as if using her as a shield.

"Sean, I've told you to leave our Polly alone. For goodness sake
she's not fifteen yet, what do you expect her to do at five o'clock in
the morning?"

"She's old enough to pull her weight now that your mother's gone.
All this schooling is going to her head. What does she need to learn to
read and write for? She'll be going in the factory sooner rather than
later if I get my way."

Sean stumbled to the sink and turned the tap on while he stuck his
head under it. Picking up a scrap of material which passed for a towel,
he rubbed his face with it and then threw it onto the draining board.

"I'm going to work. Make sure my dinner's ready when I get
home, woman!"

He picked up his pack-up tin and slammed out of the house making
the windows rattle as he went, leaving the two girls staring after him.

7

"What's up with him then?" Polly asked, knowing full well he had come home late after a skin full of ale and had fallen asleep in the living room, instead of going up to bed.

"You know he's always like this after a night out. I hate the six to two shift he's always grumpy. He'll be alright when he gets home," Laura added hopefully.

Polly doubted that very much. Things had gone from bad to worse after first her father passed away from pneumonia in 1933 and then her mother contracted diphtheria in the epidemic earlier that year in the spring of 1935. Her father had brought Sean O'Connell, an Irish immigrant, into their little house as a lodger to help pay the bills, but after Laura had married him he began to take over, bullying everyone, even her parents who had owned the house by the beck.

Too frequently now, Laura came down the stairs with a black eye or a bruised arm and body, from one of the beatings Sean had inflicted on her. It had been his fault she had lost their baby after a particularly malicious attack and both Polly and Laura wished they had never set eyes on him. Polly looked at Laura's care-worn face and moved over to hug her as she sat slumped on the stool. She tried to smile and patted Polly's hand saying, "Put the kettle on love, eh? I could do with a brew."

Polly moved over to the kettle and lifted it to see how much water was in it. She then lit the small gas ring on the stove and placed the kettle on it to boil. Looking apprehensively at her sister she said, "Do you want me to leave school now and get a job, our Laura?"

Laura shook her head decisively, "No, our mam wanted you to learn everything you could before you left, and there's only another few weeks left, so that's what you're going to do. She was adamant that you should make something of yourself and this extra year at school could set you up for life. You never know, you might want to take up teaching – you're clever enough." She pointed at the door with her thumb before adding, "He can take a running jump!"

Polly laughed, "I wish he would, our Laura, right into the Humber." They both enjoyed a rare giggle together before the kettle boiled. Once they were sat cosily at the table Polly asked, "Why don't you leave him? We could run away together. I'll soon have my school certificate. We could look after each other."

"I'm not leaving him here, Polly. This was mam and dad's house and I'm not leaving it to him to sell. He'd squander the proceeds and there'd be nothing left of dad's inheritance. You remember how proud he was when granddad left him the money. No, this house is ours, not his, and while I'm around he'll not get the better of either of us, even though he's a bit too handy with those fists of his. I'm not afraid of him."

Whether Laura had said this to stop her from worrying, Polly didn't know, but she knew that there was no love lost between the couple anymore, and if she could get away from him she would, but she couldn't leave her sister to bear the brunt of his temper. For all her bravado about not being afraid, deep down Polly knew her sister was very afraid and would never force a confrontation.

They ate a meagre breakfast of toast made from stale bread and a cup of tea, and Polly helped Laura to clean the living room after the mess Sean had made of it the night before. Later she went to get ready for school putting on her best pair of thick, black stockings which had holes in where her thumbs had gone through, and a clean pinafore over her grey dress. Laura brushed her hair for her and, as if to compensate her for Sean's bad temper, she found a nice blue ribbon to match her eyes, and then Polly went to find her plimsolls. Sean had pawned her school shoes the previous week to get some money for yet more beer. Looking out of the window she saw that there had been a sharp frost but luckily no snow to seep into the thin canvas and give her chilblains.

Picking up her books she went to give Laura a kiss before leaving to meet her friends at the corner. After extracting a promise from Laura that she would take it easier that day, she left for school promising she would be good and go straight home at dinner time. Now that she was a senior and due to leave in six weeks time, she was allowed to attend only in the morning so that she could help Laura in the afternoon. She just hoped Sean would stay out of her way when he got home.

Barton-upon-Humber was a small market town in Lincolnshire and they lived in a tiny house beside the beck, near St. Marys Church, a newer church than the smaller St. Peters which stood opposite the house. There was only a matter of yards between the two churches but St. Peters was the oldest by a couple of hundred years, and had its roots in Saxon history, but the Normans had added a tower to the top of it. St Marys was a 12th century building and much grander than the older St. Peters. The beck was fed by a spring running under St Marys and during medieval times it was said people were baptised in the water. The excess water drained off underground emerging on Butts Lane and then found its way to the sea.

The settlement itself was ancient and had been there before the Roman invasion with fragments of their pottery and coins having been dug up by archaeologists and local historians throughout recent history. Making her way up the High Street, which again gave evidence of its Saxon town planning, Polly was joined by Mary Simkins whose father owned a pastry shop on the corner of King Street. Sometimes Mary would bring something for Polly and her other friends to eat at playtime, if there had been anything left over from the shop. Mary had a plain face but a kind heart and knew that things were difficult for Polly and Laura now that her parents had gone and that awful Irishman had married into the family.

"Hello, Polly," said Mary getting into step as they hurried towards the Church School which they both attended.

Polly smiled a welcome to Mary and shivered through her thin coat. "Hello, Mary, it's a bit nippy today, isn't it? Did you do the homework Miss Backhouse gave us?"

Mary nodded in response to both questions and slipped her arm through Polly's so that she could share a little of her warmth with her friend. "I hate the winter," she said through chattering teeth.

By the time they had reached the school gates, there were four of them huddled together for warmth, Margaret and Edna Shucksmith, sisters who lived on George Street, who made up their little gang. They entered the playground just as the whistle was blowing and joined the other children as they lined up in their classes ready to enter the school. The infants went in first, followed by the juniors and then the seniors made their way to their own classroom. It was a mixed school but the boys had a separate playground as they played rougher games than the girls but it didn't stop them from climbing on top of the wall and shouting comments at the them, until one of the male teachers saw them and hoiked them down again.

Inside the school it was warm and cosy, the coal for the boilers was kept in the playground against the wall which separated the girls from the boys and in the middle of the yard were the toilet blocks, again separated for girls and boys. The school had been built in the last century when sanitation had not been much of an issue so the recent addition of the toilet blocks had been very welcome except of course in the winter when the pipes froze more often than not.

The classroom which Polly and her friends shared had a long bench where the girls sat at the front and another one at the back which accommodated the boys. Hot water pipes ran around the walls and Polly took off her plimsolls and put them on the pipes to dry out. The frost from the night before had melted to leave puddles of water in places and her thin shoes had been soaked by the time she reached the playground. Her stockings were just as bad but there was nothing she could do about that but surreptitiously slid her feet onto the pipes when she thought Miss Backhouse wasn't watching.

In the middle of the morning they were given a few minutes break and Mary produced the stale cakes her father had given her before she left home. She was always a very popular girl and even more so when she brought cakes with her, but she was generous enough to share them not only with her close friends, but with other children too. Polly closed her eyes in ecstasy as she tasted the custard tart which, although a few days old now, melted on her tongue as if it was just baked. She was growing fast and Laura said she resembled a yard of pump water, because she was so tall and thin. Polly knew she was growing because her clothes didn't fit as well as they had done and her chest was showing the signs of approaching womanhood, a fact which embarrassed her so much, she prayed she would stay flat-chested so as not to call attention to herself. Her grey dress had a large hem on it but had been let down twice this year already but her pinafore was long enough to cover her knees and preserve her modesty.

When the break was over she went back into the classroom but was called out almost immediately into the small corridor by Miss Backhouse and told to report to Miss Hewitt's office, the Headmistress of the girls section of the school. Her heart sank and her brain raced to try and think of why she had been called out specially. As far as she could remember she hadn't done anything wrong. Tentatively she knocked on Miss Hewitt's door and waited to be summoned into the inner sanctum, but instead the lady herself came to the door and smiled at Polly gesturing to her to enter.

"Ah, Miss Hardcastle, come in please."

Miss Hewitt was a middle-aged woman who had forsaken marriage and instead given her life to teaching children. Grey streaked her hair now and she wore small round spectacles. She nodded to a chair in front of her and waited for Polly to sit down. Polly perched on the edge of the high-backed chair and waited to hear what she had done wrong but instead the older lady smiled saying, "Thank   you   for coming, Polly. I've asked you here today as you are now coming up to the point of leaving us to go out into the world to earn your living. I know you have worked hard and you have justified the faith your mother put in you by becoming one of our best pupils," she paused while Polly looked intently at the floor. "Because I consider you to be of above average intelligence, I have been working behind the scenes to secure a position for you which I hope you will enjoy."

Polly looked astounded at the woman behind the desk - she hadn't expected anything like this. She had thought she would go to one of the factories in the town like the other girls, just as Laura had when she left school. There was a choice between Halls Ropery and the Elswick Hopper factory which made bicycles, or of course she could have got a job in a shop as she was good at figure work. Her thoughts were interrupted as Miss Hewitt continued.

"Sir Giles Beauchamp requires a young girl to serve in the nursery in his household. He has a new baby son and has asked me to recommend someone for the position of nursemaid. As you know he and his wife live at The Elms but you would still need to live in to fulfil your duties properly. The wage you would receive is 10 shillings per week with Saturday afternoons and all day Sunday off."

Polly's brain was racing trying to take in everything that was being said but it had been so unexpected, she couldn't form a coherent thought.

"What do you think Polly? Do you think you would like to be put forward for the position or not?"

Polly gulped before answering, "I... I don't know Miss. I would need to ask our Laura first. Can I tell you tomorrow?"

"Yes, of course but in the meantime, can I tell Sir Giles that you would be happy to work for him if your sister agrees?"

"Well, yes – I suppose so. Thank you, Miss, I'll speak to Laura this afternoon and ask her if I can do it."

"Very well, you can rejoin your class now. Come to see me first thing in the morning and let me know what your sister has decided."

Polly was dismissed and knew it but paused at the door on her way out, turned to Miss Hewitt and said, "Thank you for thinking of me Miss, I'm really pleased you think I could do it."

Miss Hewitt didn't comment but smiled as Polly closed the door. She had had high hopes for that girl but knew that she was unable to stay on at school any longer as the household needed her wages. Polly was a bright girl and a pretty one too, with one of the quickest minds she had ever had to teach. It had been a pleasure to watch her absorb her lessons so avidly. It had been her secret wish that Polly would go to a teacher training college and return to the school to help with the children. It was a pity about her parents but many people had lost relatives during the epidemic, but the greatest pity was Sean O'Connell, of whom she had heard very bad things, and the thought that Laura had married him didn't bear thinking about.

When the bell rang at lunchtime and the four friends met up to walk home, they were agog to hear what had gone on in Miss Hewitt's office. Polly told them what had been said and they were open-mouthed with awe as not one of them had been in The Elms, although they had glimpsed the interior when they had been Christmas carolling. A sum of money was always left at the door for the poor children and Polly had joined in a conspiracy with her next door neighbours when she was younger and each had gone back to the door a number of times, wearing each other's coats. From the door she had seen wall to wall carpets, beautiful thick velvet curtains, and a smell of opulence she could only guess at and dream about, in her icy bed late at night.

When she got home Laura was waiting for her and handed her a round of bread and dripping to keep her going until Sean got home from work. When Polly told her about her offer of employment from Sir Giles Beauchamp of all people, Laura was so excited she couldn't keep still.

"Oh, our Polly, what a wonderful chance for you; I know it's not teaching, but at least it's not factory work." She came round the other side of the table and hugged her sister as they danced around the kitchen together. Just then the door was flung inwards and Sean came in with a sour look on his face.

"What's going on here? I hope you've got my dinner on or you'll be for it," he grumbled as he threw his pack-up tin on the draining board. Looking at Polly he jabbed a finger at her and snarled, "I've got news for you, miss. Seeing as how you're leaving school in a few weeks, I've got you a job at the Ropery. You'll start the Monday after you leave school and no arguments, so you can stop looking at me like that."

Polly looked at Laura and burst into tears, her elation of the morning dissolved in an instant. Laura turned on her husband in anger shouting,

"Polly has come home with news of a job that her headmistress has got for her as a nursemaid."

"Well she's not taking it so there. She'll go to the Ropery like anybody else and earn a decent wage. I'm not keeping her when she's left school, Laura, so don't think I am."

Laura stood her ground as she tried to explain to him who her employer would be but he didn't want to listen and grabbed her by the arms and shook her into submission. Polly was distraught and tried to get between him and her sister only to receive a sharp kick in the shins for her pains. Howling with pain she screamed at the top of her voice and only stopped when Sean slapped her face hard with the back of his hand. There was a knock on the front door and Sean flung the sisters away from him and went to open it, realising as he did so that Polly's scream must have alerted the neighbours. Instead he came face to face with Police Constable Clayton, the local beat bobby.

"Now then, O'Connell, I was just passing and thought I heard someone screaming. What's going on, is somebody hurt in there." He tried to see past Sean into the back kitchen but couldn't as the door had slammed shut with the through draught.

Sean, now on his best behaviour, was all smiles, "Now to be sure constable there's nothing amiss, my wife has just dropped a kettle full of hot water and Polly has screamed that's all."

PC Clayton was not convinced but he couldn't very well go and look for himself without being invited in, but he was reassured when Laura came through to the hallway and repeated what her husband had said. Although she issued a belated invitation for him to come in for a cup of tea, PC Clayton declined, giving a meaningful look to Sean as he turned and left. Sean was a local troublemaker and drunk so he didn't believe for a minute that his story was true but without a complaint from anyone what was he to do?

In the back kitchen Laura was rubbing Polly's leg where a bruise was now showing.

"I'm not going to the Ropery, Laura, I'm not!" Polly hissed, "he can say what he likes but I'm gonna go to work for Sir Giles at The Elms."

"Sir Giles? The Elms?" Sean had heard her last remark and was at once all ears.

"Yes, you idiot," Laura hurled at him, "Polly has been offered a place there as a nursemaid for the young baby. If you'd just stopped and listened a minute she would have explained it, but no, you have to go in with both hands and feet and push your weight around."

"What's he gonna pay you?" Sean glared sideways at Polly waiting for an answer.

"Ten shillings with half a day Saturday and all day Sunday off," she answered reluctantly.

"Well if you take it, I want to see you cough up your board and lodge. You can keep a sixpence for yourself," he conceded.

"It's a living-in job, Sean, you won't need my money."

"You can still cough up something to repay me for all the time I've kept you," he replied meanly.

"Well that's settled then," Laura said brightly, "now let's have some dinner and try and be civilised. If you can manage it," she added pointedly looking at Sean.

When they had eaten and washed the dishes, Laura and Polly went into the small living room and put the radio on but the news was so depressing about riots in Germany and anti-Semitism they promptly turned it off again. Things were bleak enough in their own lives without listening to more bad news.

Laura pulled out some clothes that needed mending and both girls started to sew while Sean snored in an armchair which their father used to use and which Polly still regarded as his. The dark nights came in early and by four o'clock the curtains were closed and the fire banked up with slack to make it last longer. Polly got up to make a cup of tea, deliberately omitting to bring one for Sean but he woke up just as she sat down to drink hers and made her get up and pour one for him. Afterwards he went upstairs to get ready to go out and stared at Laura, daring her to make any comment about it, but she stayed quiet and waited to hear him slam the door as he left.

Once he had gone, the two girls breathed a sigh of relief and Polly began to get ready for bed. Sean had made her sleep in the kitchen as he said he had a use for her bedroom, but so far they didn't know what it was. She didn't mind, the further away from him she could get the better. The truckle bed was comfortable enough, but the blanket had seen better days. He had pawned most of her bedding to get the money for drink but the kitchen was usually warm by the fire which heated the hot water tank and it also had an oven at the side, so if she was cold outside Laura would warm a brick in it for her and it would warm her toes nicely.

In bed that night as she listened to Sean coming in the front door and stumble up the stairs, she dreamed of the imposing Victorian building which stood in its own grounds and housed Sir Giles and his family. She couldn't wait to see Miss Hewitt the following morning and tell her she would be delighted to try for the job of nursery maid.

Chapter 2

As soon as she got into school the next day Polly asked to see Miss Hewitt and was given leave to go to her office. The headmistress was pleased to see her and waited for her answer.

"I've spoken to my sister, Miss, and she says I can go and work for Sir Giles if I want to."

"And do you want to, Polly?" Miss Hewitt smiled at her young protégé.

"Yes, Miss, very much – that's if he thinks I'm suitable."

"I'm sure he will – he has asked for my recommendation and I said you would fit the bill. You are to present yourself to the back door of The Elms tomorrow morning at ten o'clock and Lady Beauchamp will ask you a few questions - afterwards you will be introduced to the other staff. Do you understand, Polly?"

"Yes, Miss. Don't worry I won't be late and thank you, Miss, for recommending me I mean."

"I'll be sorry to lose you, Polly. You have always been a good student and a credit to your class. The younger children will miss you reading stories to them too. I wish you could have gone on to a teaching position but I hope you enjoy working for Sir Giles and his family. You'd better rejoin your class now."

Polly walked back into her classroom but could think of nothing else except the interview the following morning. She dreamed of walking down the rich, carpeted corridors and looking after the baby, although she had little experience of babies so she hoped one of the other servants would help her, not knowing what a nursemaid was meant to do.

At break time she told her friends what had been decided so they made plans to meet up the following afternoon to hear how Polly's interview had gone. As it would be Saturday, Mary usually helped in her father's shop but the girls said they would meet her in the yard at the back of the shop and let her know how things went. As they walked home at lunch time each girl gave Polly advice on what she should wear or say and told her to take notice of everything she saw so that she could tell them all about it, and she promised she would do her best. As she reached Beck Hill where her familiar home stood next to the beck, she saw the Taylor's youngest children, two girls and a boy, from next door sitting on the bank and throwing stones into the water. They were huddled close to keep warm as they were wearing only thin jumpers and plimsolls, and could see that the youngest girl had been crying.

"What's the matter, Marie? Why are you crying?" Polly sat down next to them and put her arm around Marie.

"Mam and Dad are rowing again," Marie's sister, Evelyn, answered for her. "Dad's just thrown his dinner up the wall and Mam's threatened to fetch the police."

Polly looked at Marie's worried little face and pulled her close to comfort her, "Don't worry, Marie, they'll be friends again soon, they always make it up don't they?"

Marie nodded silently, a big tear dripping off the end of her nose. Polly's heart went out to the Taylor children, their parents were always at each other's throats and the eldest children didn't help much. There were nine of them altogether including the adults, their ages ranged from George who was twenty down to Marie who was seven. Many nights she had been woken up by things being thrown against the wall and voices raised in anger, but arguments were nothing new to Polly, Laura and Sean were becoming just as bad as Mr and Mrs Taylor. Just then Mrs Taylor came out and fetched them in, giving Tommy a clout as he passed her for getting his trousers muddy on the wet grass.

"Come on you lot, yer dad's gone out so yer can finish yer dinner now."

Polly let herself into the back door of her own home and found Laura peeling potatoes at the kitchen sink.

"Oh, Polly I'm glad you're back, will you go to Simpson's and get some bones for a broth. I've got some vegetables from Small's, he was selling them off cheap, but some of them are so bad I'm having to cut a lot away."

Polly dragged her coat back on and took the sixpence Laura held out to her. "I've got to be at The Elms for an interview tomorrow at ten, Laura. I don't know what I can wear though, have you any ideas?"

"We'll have a look through mam's stuff tonight maybe we can alter something to fit."

"That's a good idea, I never thought of that. Mam had some lovely dresses – you never know, one might be suitable." Polly brightened visibly at the thought and went out again, almost colliding with Sean as he came in.

"Watch where you're going you clumsy idiot," he growled as he forced his way past her into the kitchen. Thankfully, Polly was in such a good mood about the idea of altering one of her mother's dresses, she didn't react as she normally would, and let the incident pass but cast a glance at Laura through the kitchen window who shrugged despondently and carried on peeling the vegetables.

Mr Simpson, the butcher, was a middle-aged man with a roving eye for the young ladies of the village but his wife, who also worked in the shop, kept a close eye on him. Today though, she was nowhere to be seen and Mr Simpson himself came to serve Polly. She asked for some bones for broth and he winked at her as he wrapped them up in newspaper saying,

"Now then young Polly, how's your Laura these days?"

"She's alright thanks Mr Simpson except for that bloke she married of course."

Mr Simpson gave her a knowing look, "I hope he's not knocking her about is he, Polly?"

"I can't really say, Mr Simpson, but she has more bruises now than she used to, so you can draw your own conclusions."

Polly knew Mr Simpson liked a good gossip and knew if she played on his heartstrings a bit he might let her keep the bones for nothing and then she could ask for some sausage with the money. Just then Mrs Simpson came into the back of the shop and very quickly, he pushed the bones into a brown paper carrier bag and almost hurled them at Polly, winking at her to keep quiet. Polly didn't need telling twice and when Mrs Simpson approached the counter Polly asked for six links of sausage and paid for them out of the sixpence. She left the shop quickly just in case she was asked to explain about the bones to the butcher's wife, but there was no challenge and she almost ran home with her purchases swinging haphazardly in the carrier bag on her arm. When she got home Sean was ranting at Laura who sat at the kitchen table in tears and Polly rushed to her side to offer some comfort.

"What's the matter, what's going on? What have you done to her this time?" she looked accusingly at Sean.

"I've done nothing. That oh so snooty foreman at work has just given me the sack so you need to get that job tomorrow 'cos I need the money," he bellowed.

"You must have done something to get the sack, Sean; they don't get rid of people for nothing." Polly was looking at Laura for support but got only a blank expression in return.

"Come on Laura, it'll be alright, let's get dinner on and we'll all feel better."

19

"I'm off out. Where's yer purse?" he looked at Laura who nodded to the shopping bag under the kitchen sink.

He went over to the sink and found her shopping bag. He took the purse out and opened it up but there was only a shilling in it. He exploded with temper and threw it across the room just missing Polly's head.

"What've yer done with the wages I give yer last week?" he roared at Laura.

"You've been out every night Sean, and raided my purse each time, so don't start blaming me when there's nothing left." Laura answered bravely.

"Well I'm taking this shilling and there won't be anymore coming from me so what yer gonna do now?"

He stormed out of the house and Polly sat down and held Laura's hand trying to offer some grain of comfort.

"Guess what Laura. Mr Simpson gave me the bones so I bought us some sausages. We've got a penny left for a rainy day."

The incongruity of the statement made them both dissolve into laughter and after a while Laura got up to finish preparing the meal.

"We'll have the sausages to ourselves," she said to Polly, "he can lump it."

Later on in the evening there was still no sign of Sean so they drew the curtains and settled down for yet another night listening to the wireless.

The news from Spain was just as bad as that from Germany; 1934 had seen the depression hitting both countries very hard, as well as Britain, but Franco had assumed control of the army in Spain and Adolf Hitler had announced an increase in the size of the German army. Nothing looked stable in the world and when Hitler later became Chancellor and president at the same time, the politicians became pessimistic about the global outcome.

Polly hated listening to the news so they turned it off and Laura went to fetch a box containing their mother's old clothes from the spare bedroom. Inside they found just the thing for Polly to wear for her interview and set about taking in the seams. The dress was a deep shade of red with a black collar and cuffs and after a couple of hours Polly tried it on and it fitted perfectly, not even needing taking up.

"You must have grown a lot this year Polly," Laura observed. "You're nearly a young woman now. Mam and dad would have been proud of you."

"I just hope I get the job otherwise life won't be worth living. What will you do if Sean doesn't get another job?"

"I'll go out and get one myself. If all else fails I'll take in washing. Goodness knows what he did to get the sack. Maybe I'll ask around tomorrow and see what I can find out."

"Maybe Mr Taylor next door will know seeing as he works there as well."

"Christmas isn't going to be much fun this year is it? There's only five weeks to go and we don't have any money for presents," Polly said wistfully.

"Let's wait and see what happens tomorrow," Laura was the practical one in the family and being five years older than Polly she always tried to lift her spirits.

The back door slammed, shaking the house and Sean appeared in the doorway, remarkably not the worse for drink but he was breathing hard and took a quick look around before darting upstairs. They heard him moving about in the room that used to be Polly's bedroom and wondered what he was doing, but neither of them bothered too much and five minutes later he was down again.

"That looks nice Polly," he remarked looking at the made over dress. The two girls looked amazed at him as neither of them had heard a compliment from him for a very long time, not since he was trying to win Laura in fact.

"What – can't I say anything in this house?" he demanded, looking at their faces, "put the kettle on Laura I could do with a cuppa."

Both girls went into the kitchen and Polly took off her dress and hung it on a hanger off the picture rail ready for the next morning. It was quite early still but she decided to get into bed anyway, and leave the married couple to have a few minutes together. Laura had fallen out of love with Sean many months before, especially after losing her baby, and really couldn't care less whether they sat together or not, but Polly wanted to have an early night so that she would be alert the following morning ready for her interview.

Laura took the cup of tea into the living room and handed it to Sean who took it without remark, staring into the fire.

"What were you doing upstairs?" Laura asked innocently.

"Never you mind and don't go poking about up there either. I don't have to explain myself to you."

Laura looked at her husband under lowered lashes as she drank her tea and wondered what she had ever seen in him. When her father had first brought him home she was infatuated almost from the start by his dark blue eyes and long black eyelashes. He had the face of an angel but the heart of the devil, the shame of it was that she hadn't looked very deep before falling in love with him. He had been on his best behaviour, getting his feet under the table and sucking up to her mam and dad, buying drinks and presents but since her parents had died and she'd married him, he had shown his true colours alright, and now he disgusted her and she despised him with every fibre of her being. She was sure he was unfaithful too, from the knowing looks she got when she was in the town, people putting their heads close together and whispering as she passed by. He had come over from Ireland to look for work and for a time had worked as a labourer in the steelworks in Scunthorpe, but one day he had turned up at the ropery in Barton and there he had met her dad and the rest was history. He was a tall handsome man, with a muscular body and fine bones, her mam had said he had Romany blood by the looks of him, but Polly had never liked him. She seemed to be able to look through people and see their insides rather than their exterior, a talent that Laura wished she possessed too. Still, she mentally shook herself, what was done was done, and now she had to live with the consequences.

Earlier that day she had washed her hair in the kitchen sink and rinsed it with rain water from the water butt outside. She was still an attractive girl and Sean noticed her slim figure as she stretched and yawned. She stood up and Sean looked at her with that look in his eye which told her she wouldn't get much sleep that night. She wished he'd had a few drinks, he might have fallen asleep downstairs again but as she moved to the door to go upstairs, her husband stood up too and followed her. Laura would have been happy to exchange places with any one of his fancy women given half the chance.

Chapter 3

A brisk morning welcomed Polly the next day; again the frost had been heavy but the late November day was heralded by a cold blue sky. A cold day was welcome after the heat of the previous summer. Recent flooding down by Waterside and the Maltkins had caused havoc for the residents. So far the winter hadn't been too bad, and Polly hoped it would stay that way. She would have to borrow a pair of Laura's shoes to go with the dress they had altered the night before and hopefully she would have a pair of stockings that would be suitable without too many holes showing below the hemline. By nine thirty she was ready to set off for her interview. Laura hugged her and wished her luck as she set off. Her borrowed shoes and stockings were a bit big, but the dress made her feel very confident, although by the time she reached the big house, she was quaking.

The Elms was a grand house on Whitecross Street which sat on the top of a rise overlooking Baysgarth Park where there was a bandstand and a play area for children. The parkland had been given over to the council by a wealthy local family to benefit the townspeople, and a tennis court and a bowling green had been added. She could tell it was an old house as ivy covered the walls and overhung the windows but she had no idea about architecture so presumed it was Victorian as so many houses around and about were. Approaching the backdoor she was surprised to find a water pump in the back yard and the view down to the orchards was interrupted by greenhouses and lawns. There were a few steps leading down to the back door and as she was about to knock the it was opened by a plump figured lady with rosy cheeks, wearing a crisp white apron over a grey pinstriped dress.

"Hello," said Polly, "I'm Polly Hardcastle and I've been told to come here for an interview for the position of nursery maid." Her breath came quickly and she seemed to gasp the words in a hurry rather than speak them.

"Oh, right you'd better come in then. I'm Mrs Garside – the cook." She ushered Polly into the hot kitchen where another young girl stood at the Belfast sink washing dishes.

"This is Amy," Mrs Garside waved in the direction of a young girl dressed in a grey dress with a long apron which almost reached the floor. She had short brown hair and seemed a little shy but her smile lit up her face when she looked at Polly. She seemed very pleased to see someone more her own age with whom she hoped she might make friends.

"Hello Amy – I'm Polly," she introduced herself.

A tall man came into the kitchen looking full of the authority age and familiarity with his surroundings have given him. He appeared to be about sixty years old and stooped slightly, but this might have been his height rather than his age, Polly thought.

"This is Polly Hardcastle, Mr Henderson – she's come for the nursery maid's job" explained Mrs Garside.

"Ah yes, Miss Hardcastle – you are expected. Come this way." He indicated a narrow flight of stairs which led up to the ground floor of the main house. Polly felt her stomach turn over as she followed Mr Henderson up the staircase and found herself in a wide hallway which she recognised from her Christmas carolling days. Who would have thought she would ever see it from the inside she asked herself in wonder.

"Wait here," she was told and realised she wasn't expected to sit down, but to stand until summoned. Mr Henderson knocked quietly on the double doors but didn't wait for an answer before going in. The door closed behind him and Polly had the chance to look around and take in her surroundings. There was a grand staircase leading up to the first floor and everywhere was richly carpeted, although she noticed one or two places where it was going threadbare, but compared to what she was used to, it was palatial. There were so many doors leading off to different rooms, she was sure that if she got the job she would get lost. Her thoughts were interrupted by Mr Henderson coming out and saying,

"Lady Beauchamp will see you now miss." He stood aside and waited for her to step past him. Once inside the room the door closed leaving her alone with the female occupant of the room who was standing looking out of the French windows. Lady Beauchamp turned to look at Polly and took in her appearance with one sweeping glance but there was no reaction in her eyes. She was a tall lady and a lot younger than Polly had expected, with beautiful shiny black hair which was taken up in a French pleat and secured with a comb decorated with an enamel butterfly. Polly thought her the most glamorous woman she had ever seen.

"Please sit down Miss Hardcastle, thank you for coming." Her voice was soft and husky with warmth as she spoke, and Polly was momentarily reminded of her mother.

"Thank you, madam." Polly replied, hoping her response had been appropriate. She had discussed with Laura that morning how she should address her prospective employer and they had decided that 'madam' sounded respectful.

Polly sat down on the chair opposite Lady Beauchamp and immediately sank into the rich comfort it offered. Her mind started to imagine the rest of the house and had to force herself to concentrate on the matter in hand.

"Now, Polly, it is Polly, isn't it?" the question was rhetorical but Polly nodded and Lady Beauchamp continued, "I understand you are interested in becoming nursery maid to my baby son and that you will be leaving school at Christmas when you are fifteen. Is this correct?"

"Yes madam. I would like to hear more about the job though."

"Well, you will be responsible for making sure the nursery is clean and tidy at all times and you will also cover for Jane Brown who is our nanny. She will take her full day off on Friday and her half day on Saturday morning. She will instruct you on the routine she has established. You will be expected to deliver meals to the nursery for baby Michael and also for Jane. My husband has two other children from his first marriage but they are at boarding school at the moment and you will meet them at Christmas. Your room will be on the top floor in what used to be the servants quarters but since the last war we have only employed a skeleton staff and most of them live in the town."

Polly listened intently to Lady Beauchamp's instructions and nodded her understanding.

"How old is your baby, miss, er, I mean madam?" Polly faltered.

"He is almost nine months now. He is a big strong boy and loves to play. Do you have experience of children Polly?"

"Not as such, madam. I'm the youngest in our family. I live with my sister and her husband as my mam and dad have both died, but I've looked after my neighbour's children. There are nine of them altogether so I'm not without experience."

"Mostly your duties will be fetching and carrying and cleaning but I'm sure Jane will need you to help her occasionally. Are you still interested in the position, Polly? My husband tells me that Miss Hewitt spoke very highly of you."

"Ooh, yes please madam. I'd love to come and work for you – if you'll have me that is."

"I think we can say we are mutually suited, Polly. Would you like to meet Michael now?"

"That would be lovely madam. Thank you."

Lady Beauchamp moved to the bell pull and tugged it to alert Henderson to come back into the room. He appeared like an apparition taking Polly by surprise.

"Henderson, please inform Jane that I wish to see her with Michael immediately."

"Yes madam," Henderson replied obediently.

Polly thought that Jane must have been hovering nearby as the door seemed to open again almost as soon as Henderson had left and a woman holding a fractious baby walked into the room. She was a skinny, youngish woman with a sour face who seemed to struggle unnecessarily with her burden, who in turn began to cry at being held so roughly.

The introductions were made amid cries and protests from Michael but when Polly could stand the struggle no longer, she stood up and held her arms out to him and he almost leapt into them, bringing a spiteful look from Jane. Once in Polly's arms he immediately became quiet and seemed fascinated with her hair, taking big handfuls and trying to put it into his wet little mouth. Polly laughed and he chuckled as he buried his head in her neck and dribbled onto her freshly ironed collar.

Lady Beauchamp didn't miss the look which Jane gave Polly but didn't remark upon it. Polly sat down again putting Michael on her lap and he seemed happy with his new position as he surveyed the room and his mother. He held his arms out to her and she picked him off Polly's lap and carried him to the window.

"Jane," she said turning back into the room, "why don't you take Polly upstairs while I've got Michael and show her the nursery and where she is to sleep."

"Yes madam," was the only reply Jane made and stood up and waited for Polly to follow her.

"Please come back, when you've finished, Polly, there's a few more details I'd like to go over with you."

Polly nodded and followed Jane back into the hallway and then up the grand staircase, which she had glimpsed through the open door when she was a child. Jane was very quiet and turned left at the top of the first flight of stairs. Polly tried to draw her into conversation but only received curt replies so she waited until they were in the nursery.

She stood in the middle of the room and looked at the baby's cot and highchair. There was a nursing chair in the corner and the window looked out onto the back garden. Polly thought it was a beautiful room and said so to Jane who immediately turned on her spitefully, her eyes narrowing as she spat, "If you ever show me up again young lady, you'll be sorry. Taking Michael off me like that in front of madam. You made me look foolish in front of her. She'll think I can't handle a baby."

"I'm sorry I thought I was being helpful. I didn't mean anything by it. Babies can be difficult sometimes..." Polly's apology tailed off as Jane's face showed no sign of forgiveness.

"Well, be warned. I won't have you undermining me. Your job is to fetch and carry so don't get ideas above your station, my girl."

"No, of course, I'm sorry."

Jane brushed past her as if in dismissal and showed her via a connecting door into a room which she used as her own sitting room cum bedroom. In one corner there was a small single bed with a metal frame, neatly made up and a table in the middle of the room with fresh flowers in a small vase in the centre.

"This is my room so you don't come in here at all. When you cover for me on my night off there is a truckle bed against the wall in the nursery – you can use that. Now I'll show you up to your own room, it's on the next floor."

They went out of the nursery and up another narrow staircase to the upper floor where Polly was to sleep. Jane opened one of the doors on the landing and stood back to let her in. Again there was a single bed and a chest of drawers with a mirror over it. A small window looked out on the back of the house, much the same as Jane's had. Polly presumed correctly that at one time these small rooms would have been used by the many servants that the family employed, but now they were vacant as domestic staff was so difficult to come by since the war.

"This is a very nice room I'm sure I'll be comfortable here," Polly said to Jane who shrugged as if she couldn't care less if she was or not. Polly noticed that there was running water plumbed into the room which was a great relief as many big houses still used wash basins filled by fetching water up from the depths of the house. Yes, she thought to herself, I shall be very comfortable here.

Turning round she noticed that Jane had left her alone so she quietly closed the door and made her way back down the stairs to find

Lady Beauchamp. She knocked politely on the sitting room door and was surprised that Jane opened it for her and she was looking bad tempered.

"Ah, Polly dear please come in. Jane, take Michael back to the nursery." Jane walked past Polly with Michael in her arms and closed the door behind her. A moment passed and then Lady Beauchamp opened the door quickly only to find that Jane and Michael were still hovering outside the door, guessing that she had been waiting to overhear what was being said.

"I said, thank you, Jane. There's no need to wait, please take Michael back to the nursery as I asked." Lady Beauchamp left Jane in no doubt that she was displeased to find her still there and closed the door sharply.

She turned and smiled at Polly, "I don't think Jane is too happy about you joining us, Polly. She's been here about three months and between you and me she was my only choice. Would you believe the agency only sent me Jane. They said there were no other applicants. I found that hard to believe but it's so difficult to get staff these days. Now, I want to ask you whether you would consider starting immediately. I know you haven't left school yet, but I really need you to start now rather than waiting until Christmas. I'm sure we can work something out with Miss Hewitt, what do you say?"

Polly was taken aback by the suggestion and didn't know what to say. "I'll have to ask my sister madam, but I should think if Miss Hewitt says it's alright, then I don't see any reason why not."

"Good girl, I hoped you'd say that. Henderson will be here in a minute and I want him to give you your uniform and if it needs altering perhaps you can do that before you begin your duties. I believe my husband has already spoken to Miss Hewitt about wages, so if there's nothing else Polly, I'll wait to hear from you regarding your starting date. To give you a chance to sort yourself out, I think a week on Monday will be best – what do you say?"

"That will be ideal Miss. I'll leave a message with Mr Henderson if Miss Hewitt says I must stay at school."

"Thank you, Polly. You may go now."

As if on cue Henderson opened the door to show Polly out and took her down to the kitchen again where a dark blue dress with a white apron waited for her on the large, scrubbed pine table. Mrs Garside smiled and Amy appeared pleased that she would be joining them. Mr

Henderson wrapped the clothes in a brown paper parcel for her and tied it with thin string.

"We'll see you soon then, Polly," said Mrs Garside as she opened the back door for her and she waved to them as she walked out into the clean fresh air. She hadn't noticed how warm it had been in the house until she came out again and relished the thought of being warm all the time inside the house instead of freezing to death while waiting to use the outside toilet at home.

She almost ran to Mary's house and the others were waiting for her to hear all the gossip. Their eyes were round when she told them about the plush carpets and curtains, and about her own little room at the top of the house. They were all happy for her but said they would miss her if she left school early. Polly thanked them and said she would miss them too but was hoping Laura would say 'yes' to her as she couldn't wait to start work and start earning some money. If Sean O'Connell thought he was going to get all of it he had another think coming.

Chapter 4

When she arrived home both Laura and Sean were in the kitchen waiting to hear how it had gone. When she explained about leaving school Sean was all for it so Laura said it would be alright with her too, although she looked a little unhappy about it, in fact she looked very unhappy indeed but Polly couldn't ask her about it until later when Sean had gone out.

Much to their disappointment he didn't go out until after tea so Polly had to hold her curiosity in check but once the door had slammed and they heard him walking through the passage which separated them from next door Polly said,

"Well! What's up Laura? You've looked really upset all day."

Laura smiled bleakly at her sister and said "It's *him* Polly. I'm sure he's been pinching things and stashing them away in your old bedroom. I'm scared to death the police come round and find whatever it is."

Polly put her hand over her mouth and opened her eyes wide in response to the news.

"Oh, Laura, no! What's he been pinching? Is that why he went straight upstairs last night before he came in here?"

"Yes. He told me to stay out of the bedroom and when I asked why he gave me a backhander and told me to mind my own business. So I know he's been up to no good."

"Shall we go up and have a look while he's out?" Polly suggested with a look of devilment in her eyes.

"No, he's locked the door so it won't do any good. Anyway, I don't want another thump, do I?" Laura looked forlornly in the mirror over the sideboard. "I look more like thirty nine than nineteen. I wish I never set eyes on Sean O'Connell, I really do."

To take her sister's mind off things, Polly suggested they get to work on the uniform she'd been given at The Elms. They undid the brown paper parcel and found two dresses and three aprons inside and both dresses needed taking in to fit Polly's slim figure. When they had finished that they put their heads together to try and work out how they were going to manage to feed themselves until Polly was paid.

"It's just as well I'll be starting work soon otherwise we'd starve" Polly remarked. "Have you thought any more about getting a job our Laura?"

"Sean won't let me. He's funny like that. You'd think he would be pleased with an extra pay packet," she replied. "He seems to have got it into his head that wives shouldn't go out to work but if he's not earning I don't seem to have much choice. Anyway I'm off to the Labour Exchange on Monday and see what there is, if anything."

"Maybe he'll get a job soon and we'll be alright again. I'll ask him if he's tried the boatyard down Waterside" Laura offered in an effort to cheer her sister up.

"I don't think anyone will employ him. They all know what he's like. I wish I knew what he was up to though."

Just then the front door opened and closed and they heard someone going into the spare bedroom upstairs. There seemed to be more than one pair of feet and Laura turned the wireless down and they heard muttering so there was obviously more than one person up there. A few minutes later and they heard footsteps descending the stairs and the front door close. They were surprised that Sean put his head round the door and waved a ten shilling note at Laura who couldn't believe her eyes.

"Where on earth did you get that?" she asked incredulously.

"That's for me to know," he said proudly and handed over the note for Laura to hold, but snatched it back again almost immediately saying, "I'm off to the pub. See you later."

"Sean, please don't drink it all away, we need money for next week." Laura could hear the pleading in her voice and it sounded pathetic even to her but he ignored her and went out.

To her relief he came back two hours later when Polly was in bed and handed over seven shillings and sixpence, having drunk the rest with his cronies in the Sloop Inn, opposite the rope works. Although he was unsteady on his feet, he was far from drunk so Laura thanked her lucky stars and put the money in her purse, silently planning to hide some of it the next day.

The weather stayed cold but bright, and the two girls decided to go for a walk the following afternoon while Sean was sleeping off his dinner. He seemed to be in good spirits since his dealings the night before and they were happy to leave him alone snoring in their father's chair. They decided to walk through the town and go down to the waters edge at a place they called Point where the rope works bordered them on their right and houses on their left. At the end was the Humber bank and they could watch the ships going up and down the river carrying their cargoes far and wide. The boat yard stood empty of workers as it was Sunday but there were quite a few people around taking advantage of the dry weather. Polly shuddered to think how close she had come to being employed in the long low buildings of the rope works, where people spliced ropes on machines and reworked old ropes to make new ones. Halls Rope Works housed the longest rope walk in the world but both Polly and Laura were glad they never saw it from the inside.

For a long peaceful moment they watched as the tide slowly ebbed and the seagulls landed to pick up whatever food they found lying around, and then they turned back to go home. As they were entering Fleet Gate they caught sight of Mr Taylor, their next door neighbour. Laura waved to him and they caught up with him a few seconds later.

"Hello Mr Taylor, how are you?" she asked. He was a middle-aged man with auburn hair and a thick, bristly moustache. He had keen sharp eyes but by and large was friendly enough, even though he and Mrs Taylor argued a lot, it was usually only when they'd each had a bit to drink.

"Now then young ladies, out for a walk are you? Where's that husband of yours Laura?"

"He's at home, Mr Taylor. I was hoping you could tell me how he came to lose his job?" she asked outright. No good beating about the bush, she wanted to know why Sean had been sacked.

"Happen you'd best ask him love," Mr Taylor sniffed as he answered.

"He won't tell us, Mr Taylor. Was he fighting again?" Polly interceded for her sister.

Mr Taylor stopped and searched his pocket for his handkerchief and blew his nose before answering, "We managed to stop him before he pushed the foreman under one of the machines. He'd had several warnings for poor work, Laura, and when the foreman told him off he picked up a big spanner and threatened him with it. They started to grapple with each other and Sean's bigger than the foreman and pushed him towards one of the big machines. We only just managed to separate them in time. The boss got to hear about it and sacked him on the spot. He was given his wages and he went."

Laura started open-mouthed, "He was paid before he left. Are you sure, Mr Taylor?"

"Aye, I am that lass. I saw him go into the office and he was carrying a brown wages envelope when he came out."

"Thanks Mr Taylor, I'm grateful to you. Don't tell him I was asking will you?"

"No, I'll not do that, lass. We don't normally speak to each other anyway, even in the pub. He has his mates and I have mine."

Having said all he was going say, Mr Taylor turned and walked away leaving Polly and Laura speechless at Sean's callousness in not giving Laura any money for housekeeping out of his last wages. Making out Polly would have to support the family was just his way of being nasty. By the time they arrived back home Laura was seething with anger but Polly tried to calm her down and pointed out that if she said anything to him, both of them would come off worse and at least she had seven and six for next week's housekeeping which was more than she normally had. Laura wasn't convinced as she knew Sean would be in her purse at the first opportunity and take the money back when he needed a drink.

As it was, he had gone out when they got home and hadn't returned even by the time Polly left for school the next day. She was nervous about speaking to Miss Hewitt about leaving for good on Friday but as it turned out, by the time she had plucked up the courage to speak to her, she had been summoned anyway. Lady Beauchamp had written a note to Miss Hewitt regarding Polly's suitability for the post of nursery maid, and Miss Hewitt complimented her on doing well at her interview, and gave her the permission she needed to leave school with her School Certificate should she need it in the future.

The week flew by and by the time Friday came she was looking forward to packing away her books and saying goodbye to her friends, not that she wouldn't see them again of course, but as a working girl her spare time would be limited. She arranged with her friends to see them as often as she could and maybe even go to one of the church tea dances. Maybe she could persuade Laura to go with her. So with mixed feelings and after receiving her leaving certificate from school on her final day, she walked home for the last time as a schoolgirl with her three friends. Mary had brought cakes for the occasion and this time they weren't even stale, thanks to her dad who had allowed her to choose some from the shop that morning.

The weekend had passed too quickly for Polly as she stood at the back door of The Elms on the following Monday and prepared to knock. Before she could do so the door was opened by Mrs Garside who laughed and told her that now she was an employee she didn't have to knock. Amy was polishing the range cooker and Mr

Henderson looked as if he was ironing a newspaper which Polly found amazing. When she asked about it Mr Henderson told her that the gentry always insisted on having the newspaper ironed as it pressed out any creases and made it easier to read. It was only seven o'clock, but the resident staff had been up and working for hours and were well on with their allotted tasks. Amy was instructed to take Polly upstairs to her room and help her get settled which she was only too pleased to do. As they passed the nursery they could hear Michael crying and Jane's voice anxiously raised and trying to placate him but the more she raised her voice the worse he cried. Amy tutted meaningfully and looked at Polly with a look that spoke volumes and they hurried on up the stairs to Polly's room.

"My room is next to yours," she volunteered as she opened the door. "It will be lovely to have someone to talk to again. The last girl who had this job didn't last five minutes. She was needed at home urgently and had to leave. Mrs Garside's a widow and lives in her own house up Caistor Road so she hasn't far to come. The nanny lives in as you know."

Polly put her cheap cardboard suitcase on the bed and began to unpack her uniform which Laura had carefully ironed for her the night before.

"How long have you been here, Amy?" she asked.

"Two years now. I'm hoping to be promoted to maid but Mrs Garside says I'm a bit too clumsy, but I'm sure I could do it."

"I'm sure you could too," Polly replied kindly and Amy beamed at her.

"You'd best get ready then. I'll leave you to get changed and then you'd better report to that Jane downstairs as soon as you're ready."

It was obvious by her manner and the way she spoke of Jane that no love was lost between them, but for now Polly held her tongue and changed into her uniform. The colour suited her and made her eyes seem even bluer, so she confidently went to the mirror and fixed her apron and cap in place. Her thick dark hair had been tamed and fastened in a bun by Laura that morning and Polly hoped she would be able to repeat the process for the rest of the week. Once she was satisfied with her appearance, she presented herself in the nursery and waited for her instructions from Jane who immediately ordered her downstairs to prepare breakfast for her and Michael.

The morning went quickly as she was kept on the go by Jane telling her to fetch this and carry that, so it was with relief that her own lunch time arrived. She was to eat in the kitchen with the others and that included the gardener, Ned and his apprentice, a young boy called Jim. They were a father and son team who came in every day to tend the garden and do any other odd jobs which might be necessary and they seemed to be fully employed with a house and garden of this size. Polly was asked endless questions about herself and her family which she answered truthfully but left out as much about Sean as she could. She in turn asked about her colleagues and also about the two boys who were away at boarding school.

It appeared that from his first marriage Sir Giles had two older boys Martin who was seventeen, and Christopher who was fifteen. Their mother had died five years previously and three years after that Sir Giles had remarried and Michael had been born. The staff seemed to be happy in their work as they didn't see much of Sir Giles as he had business interests which took him away for a large part of the time, and Lady Beauchamp was a kind and considerate employer. When the boys came home the house came to life, she was told, and they would be home in two weeks time, ready for Christmas. Polly looked forward to meeting them and hoped they would like her in return.

Chapter 5

On the Saturday afternoon of her first week Polly went back to Beck Hill to see Laura who was delighted to see her as they had barely been separated all their lives. Polly felt odd letting herself in by the back door and entering the familiar kitchen, she felt like a stranger, as if she didn't belong anymore. Laura made tea for them and asked her all about her new job and they were well into a description of Jane and her efforts to demoralise Polly, when Sean came in. He took in the cosy scene and immediately tried to come between the sisters.

"I hope you've brought me some money!" he jabbed a finger at Polly."Hello to you too, Sean," she answered calmly, "how nice to see you. How have you been?" Polly's sarcasm wasn't lost on Laura and she started to giggle but one threatening look from her husband wiped the smile off her face. "You can stop being clever just because you're working for the big wigs now. Just give me the money you owe me."

"I don't owe you any money Sean O'Connell and if I did I'd give it to Laura, that way I'd know it would be spent on essential things and not beer." Polly's temper was rising by the minute but she was afraid that Laura would bear the brunt of the exchange so she fished out a shilling from her purse and threw it at him.

"There, that's all I've got. I have to pay for my uniform so until I have, there's nothing more for the likes of you."

Sean caught the shilling and pocketed it looking at Laura saying "Where's my tea?"

"In the oven, it's been ready for two hours but you weren't here. If it's dried up that's your fault," she answered and went to the oven at the side of the fire and took out a dish of corned beef stew holding the metal dish with a tea towel. It was a tasty but cheap way of making vegetables go further and she ladled some on a plate for him.

He grunted and sat down opposite Polly who screwed up her nose at him and stood up.

"Come on Laura let's leave him to eat on his own. We'll have a chat in the sitting room."

"I'm off out when I've eaten this and I don't know when I'll be back," Sean directed the statement to Laura and completely ignored Polly.

The sisters took their cup of tea into the sitting room and switched on the wireless to listen to some music. Laura sighed as she started humming the tunes, "I really miss going to dances. Sean never takes me anywhere."

"Well we could go to one of the sixpenny hops at the Assembly Rooms the next time there's one on, or there's the Odd Fellows Hall. Now I'm working I could pay for us to get in, what do you say Laura, shall we?"

Laura pulled a face saying, "Sean wouldn't like it Polly. He doesn't like me to go out without him."

"Serve him right if you did," Polly said as loud as she could, hoping Sean would hear, but there was no noise from the kitchen except the sound of a spoon scraping on an enamel dish. Eventually they heard him go upstairs to get changed then he left without a word to either of them. Polly relaxed and looked hard at Laura who seemed to have become quiet and withdrawn.

"Are you alright our Laura?" she asked, slipping easily back into her usual mode of speech. "Has he been hitting you again?"

"Yes I'm alright Polly, and no, he hasn't been hitting me, at least not hard the way you mean, but I get lonely without you. I wish you could come home every night."

"Has he been pinching things again?" Polly asked.

"He's always up to something. He's got work as a gravedigger up at the cemetery and starts on Monday so at least he'll be earning again. Just as well with Christmas coming. It's only two weeks away Polly and I haven't a clue what to do about dinner. Will you be able to come home?"

"Yes, I've been meaning to tell you but I forgot. I've been given Christmas Day and Boxing Day off but I have to be back by eight o'clock on Boxing Day night, but that will give us plenty of time together won't it?"

She smiled at Laura and received a hug in return. "I've really missed you this week Polly. Sean's hardly been here and when he is, he brings really rough fellows here and they frighten me to death some of 'em." Polly didn't really know what to say to make Laura feel better. She knew from experience that Sean liked to stir up trouble somewhere and he often joined in the fights between the Soutergater's and the Beck Hillers. Soutergate was only across the road from the Beck but the children had fought each other for years and occasionally the men joined in when they were drunk enough. Sean revelled in violence and she could tell that Laura was at her wits end with money worries and wondering when the police were going to be knocking on the door to arrest him. The neighbours would have a field day twitching curtains and gossiping.

"I know," Polly said jumping up, "let's push the settee back against the wall like we used to when mam and dad were here, and have a dance to the music."

Laura brightened up, and started to push the settee and chairs back against the wall making more room for them to move, then taking the lead, she and Polly danced around the small room laughing at their own antics. It was quite late when they finally went to bed, exhausted by their exertions and it felt strange to Polly to be sleeping in her little bed again even if it was only for one night. She couldn't believe how quickly she had settled in at The Elms and how much she missed the little room of her own on the top floor.

In the morning the two girls went to St Peter's church which Polly didn't like as much as St Mary's as there always seemed to be a dead crow lying outside the door as she went in. The atmosphere of the old stone and wooden pews more than made up for it though, and she enjoyed the service as they joined in with the carols. Sean never came to this church as he was brought up a Catholic but didn't practice his religion anymore. He was content to lie in his bed and sleep off the excesses of the night before, although this hadn't stopped him from unlocking the small bedroom and stashing something else away until he could sell it.

The weekend seemed to go even quicker than the previous week and in no time at all Polly found herself saying goodbye to Laura and then broke the news that she wouldn't be able to come back the next week as the boys would be home from boarding school and she had been asked to work her weekend off. Laura was disappointed which was why Polly had waited until the last minute to tell her, but as it meant more money for Polly she knew she couldn't be selfish and after one final hug she let her go.

When she arrived back at The Elms, she was disconcerted to find that Lady Beauchamp had left instructions for Henderson to show Polly into the sitting room where she wanted to speak to her. Polly was alone nervously waiting for her employer when the door opened and both Sir Giles and his wife entered. They looked a little worried themselves and Polly was sure she was going to be given the sack but relaxed a little when Lady Beauchamp smiled at her.

"Good evening, Polly," said Sir Giles. This was the first time he had spoken to her directly and she felt as if she ought to curtsey or something but didn't know what so she just said "Good evening, sir," in reply and waited for him to speak again.

He went to stand in front of the beautiful Adams fireplace which had a roaring coal and log fire burning brightly in the hearth and then turned and spoke to her again.

"It has come to our attention that Jane, is finding it difficult to cope with Michael. Have you noticed anything at all out of the ordinary?"

"No not really sir. Jane keeps me busy one way or another during the day so I don't really spend a great deal of time with Michael but I've heard him crying a little in the mornings sometimes – but babies do, don't they?"

"Yes, they do, Polly. What I'm trying to say is have you seen her smack Michael at all?"

Polly looked surprised at the question and thought carefully before answering, "No sir, I haven't seen her as such but I've noticed something about the way she speaks to him."

"And how might that be Polly?" asked Lady Beauchamp twisting her hands nervously as she spoke.

"Well she's very sharp with him, and although I've never seen her smack him, he seems to be a little afraid of her, madam."

"Polly, I want you to keep a closer eye on Jane from now on and if you see anything which you might be concerned about, I want you to come and tell me immediately. Is that clear?"

"Yes, madam of course, but I don't think Jane hurts baby Michael, she just gets a bit flustered and doesn't know how to handle him."

"Thank you, Polly that will be all. I don't normally ask my employees to spy on their colleagues but in this case, Michael's safety is paramount. I hope you understand that."

"Yes madam. I'll certainly do my best."

Polly went up to her bedroom and wondered what had prompted the interview she had just had with her employers. She went to Amy's room and knocked on the door but there was no answer so she went down the back stairs to the kitchen but was told that Amy had gone out to see some friends who she used to be in the orphanage with. She didn't like to ask Mr Henderson in case he thought she was gossiping so she went back to her room and resolved to ask Amy the following day.

When she presented herself the following morning in the nursery, Jane was sitting in the nursing chair looking out into the garden.

Michael was in his cot still fast asleep so Polly had no reason to go and look at him but received her orders from Jane as usual.

Over the next few days and with the instructions from Sir Giles and Lady Beauchamp ringing in her ears, she took special notice of Michael's wellbeing and noticed that he slept later in the mornings than he had during her first week there and when he was awake he seemed lethargic. When she mentioned it to Jane she was told to mind her own business and get on with cleaning the nursery and washing nappies, but it wasn't until the following Friday when she had Michael all to herself that she noticed he was more alert than the previous day. Jane was spending her day and a half off with her cousin who lived in the nearby village of Barrow so Polly was at liberty to play with Michael during this time.

As usual in the late afternoon and early evening he was taken downstairs to spend some time with his parents and then later he had his last feed before being put down for the night. Polly kept her observations and suspicions to herself when questioned regarding Jane's conduct as she wanted to be sure of herself before she spoke up. She fed Michael and changed his nappy and then turned the lights down until there was a cosy glow in the room and he gradually fell asleep. Polly couldn't understand how he could be so lethargic when Jane looked after him but totally bright and breezy when she looked after him herself. Once he was asleep she took a deep breath and moved towards the nanny's private quarters and tried the door – it was locked. Undeterred she searched the drawers and cupboards for anything which might support her theory that Jane was giving him a sleeping draught of some kind at night to keep him quiet, but she found nothing.

She couldn't very well force the lock but instead thought about asking Mr Henderson for a spare key if there was one, but without proof she felt uncomfortable about going that far. Standing in the middle of the room she peered into Michael's cot and looked at his cherubic face and tucked his hand under the covers thinking what a beautiful little boy he was when the door to the nursery opened and Jane stood there staring at her. Polly was thankful she hadn't turned up a few minutes earlier while she was trying the door but still looked up guiltily.

"Hello, Jane, have you forgotten something?" Polly whispered, trying to cover her nervousness.

"Yes, I promised I would take my cousin something, and I forgot. We're going out for the evening and they are waiting for me outside. Go and get yourself a cup of tea. I need to go into my room for a few minutes."

Polly wondered why she needed to get her out of the way just to go into her room, but daren't argue with her and turned to leave. She promised herself she wouldn't be more than a few minutes but Amy delayed her in the kitchen and when she came back Jane had gone. She tried the door to her room again, but it was still locked and so she was forced to abandon her idea for the time being. She wasn't left to dwell on the matter for long as the front doorbell rang and there was a noise from the downstairs hallway as Martin and Christopher announced their arrival back from boarding school.

Mrs Garside had left them a couple of plates of sandwiches and cakes and Amy made them some tea but Polly was not introduced to them until the following morning when she had bathed and dressed Michael. He had woken as he usually did when Polly had looked after him, in a very good humour and she noticed the difference in him straight away. She took him with her down to the kitchen to get his feed ready and Amy held him on her knee while Polly prepared it.

She was just spooning some rusk and milk into his mouth when a tall gangling youth entered the kitchen looking for Mrs Garside. He looked to be about fifteen or sixteen and Polly thought he must be Christopher who was just a bit older than her, and this was confirmed by the appearance of an older boy who pushed Christopher out of the way as he entered the kitchen.

"Should you be doing that here?" he asked looking pointedly at Polly. "We always had our meals in the nursery," he stated.

"Don't be such a cad, Martin," his brother said. "She's not doing any harm is she? Anyway, Michael looks happy enough."

This was true enough as he spluttered his rusk down his chin and wriggled in Polly's arms to reach out to his older brother.

"Hello, you must be Jane," Christopher said politely. "I'm Christopher and this is my older, uglier brother Martin." Martin cuffed him but laughed off the joke.

"How do you do, but I'm not Jane, I'm Polly and I'm not the nanny, I'm just the nursery maid."

Martin looked down his nose at her but didn't speak, unlike Christopher who sat opposite his baby brother and distracted him while Polly tried to feed him.

Martin went back upstairs to find Mr Henderson and left Christopher with Polly and Amy. He seemed chatty and not at all stuck up like his brother, Polly thought and when Michael had finished his breakfast, his brother picked him up and took him back upstairs with him leaving Polly to clear away.

"I think he likes you," Amy said looking knowingly at Polly.

"Who does, Michael? Well I hope so, if he didn't he might cry all the time like he did with Jane when I first came," Polly answered unwittingly.

"No, silly – Master Chris - he likes you. I could tell by the way he looked at you and stayed while you fed Michael."

Polly was amazed and refused to accept it but she blushed anyway. "No, you're mistaken Amy. You've made it up," but as she was denying it, she blushed bright red.

"Master Chris is a nice lad, but I can't stand Master Martin," Amy confided, "He's a snob and a bit of a bully too. He'll try to push you around Polly if you aren't careful."

"I'd like to see him try. My brother-in-law is a bully and he hasn't got the better of me yet." Polly answered bravely but in reality her heart sank at the thought of someone bringing more confrontation into her life. She had enjoyed her first few weeks at The Elms so much, except for Jane's pettiness of course, and she hoped Martin wasn't going to spoil things for her.

She went back to the nursery again via the back stairs and started to clean and tidy the room, waiting to be summoned to fetch Michael back for his morning nap but to her surprise it was Christopher who brought him back to her himself.

"I think he's a bit tired of us now," he laughed and handed the baby back to Polly.

Polly sniffed his nappy and smiled saying, "I think you mean he needs changing, don't you?"

"You've caught me out, Polly. Yes, he's all yours now."

She took the baby and sat him down on the nursery rug while she went to the linen cupboard to get a clean nappy and was surprised when Christopher was still there when she returned.

"Don't mind me," he said, "I'll stay and chat for a while if that's alright?"

"As long as you let me carry on with my duties, I don't want to get into trouble already. I've only been here a few weeks." Polly answered as she looked over her shoulder at him.

"We haven't been home since the new nanny started so we didn't know who was who. What's the nanny like?" Christopher's curiosity amused her. He reminded her of one of the Taylor boys. George Taylor used to be a great friend of Laura's until Sean O'Connell had turned her head, and Polly wished he would still come calling like he used to but when Laura had married Sean, he had seemed very hurt and they hadn't seen much of him since.

Bringing herself out of her reverie, she was about to answer his question regarding Jane when the lady herself walked into the room. She seemed startled to see Christopher sat talking to Polly and it flustered her into snapping at the younger girl.

"I hope you're not wasting this young man's time, girl. It's a good job I came back when I did otherwise you'd be spending all day idling about instead of attending to your work."

Polly stood open-mouthed, not sure what to say and Christopher stood up to explain.

"No, please don't blame Polly. She's been here working all morning and I've just brought Michael back to have his nappy changed. I'm Christopher Beauchamp by the way – I'm assuming your Jane, Michael's nanny?"

Jane was taken completely by surprise by his defence of Polly and back-pedalled as much as she could by trying to ingratiate herself. Polly resumed changing Michael's nappy and then ignored the other woman as much as she could until Christopher left, satisfied that he had deflected trouble away from her. When the door closed, Jane stalked past Polly and unlocked the door to her room, taking her bag with her and closed the door on them. It was time for Polly to hand Michael back into the nanny's care but was reluctant to do so. She had enjoyed looking after him and was doubly determined to get to the bottom of Jane's apparent inability to care for him properly.

Chapter 6

Polly was kept on the go from morning till night up until Christmas Eve when the tree had been decorated in the large hallway. It was so tall a step ladder had to be brought in and Martin was handed the angel to sit at the very top but at the last minute he changed his mind and asked Polly if she would do it. She was a little apprehensive as up until that minute Martin had been very distant and his manner more threatening than friendly, but Amy was with her and Christopher too, so she felt safe enough in their company.

"Come on, Polly," Martin enthused, "take my hand and I'll help you up the steps. You can have the honour as the new member of staff this year to sit the angel at the top of the tree."

As she was climbing the steps he found an excuse to send Amy for more paper to make paper chains and then asked Christopher to find some paste to stick them together. Polly stood on the top step of the ladder and felt very alone at that moment. When he was sure they weren't being watched, Martin held Polly's ankles and she immediately went rigid, afraid he was going to tip her off the steps.

"No, Master Martin, please be careful. You'll make me fall," she hissed at him.

"Don't be silly, I'm just helping you, that's all," he replied.

She reached out to put the angel at the top of the tree and as she succeeded she felt Martin running his hands up her legs as he held onto her. He went further than she thought necessary and gasped at his audacity and swung round to rebuke him but toppled over in the process. As she twisted to get away from him his hands he grabbed her thighs and she found herself being hugged tightly and slid very slowly down the length of his body. She saw him smirk at her as he freed his hands from her dress and her face turned bright red in response.

"How dare you," she pushed him away, "it's a good job your mother's not here or I'd tell her about you," she said as she smoothed her dress down.

Out of the corner of her eye she saw Christopher come back followed by Amy who had found the paper she had been looking for. Polly must have looked flustered as he remarked, "Are you alright, Polly? You look a little out of breath."

"Yes thank you. I'm fine." She gave Martin a black look and began tidying up around the tree, turning her back on all of them so that they couldn't see how angry she was.

Martin decided they didn't need the glue or paper for more chains after all and Polly used this as an excuse to go back to the kitchen and stay there until it was time for her to get her things together for her short holiday with Laura and Sean.

As she was coming down the back stairs dressed in her coat and carrying a small bag of presents she had bought, she was surprised to find Martin lying in wait for her. The stairs were fairly narrow and permitted only one person at a time either going up or coming down, so when he stood his ground and refused to move, she didn't know what to say but tried being polite.

"Excuse me, I'm leaving now but I'll be back on Boxing Day. I hope you have a happy Christmas Master Martin."

He still didn't move or answer her so she took a deep breath and moved towards him. He moved to stand sideways on the stairs as if to let her pass but her bag and coat prevented her from moving by him without touching him. As she faced him he gave her a salacious smile and pushed himself against her as she passed. She wanted the floor to open up and swallow her as he pressed himself against her and planted a wet kiss on her lips.

"Please don't do that again," she gasped as he let her go, "or I really will have to speak to your mother about your conduct."

"Oh, Polly, don't be such a prude. Anyway, as the future master of the house, it's my right to claim a kiss at Christmas from the domestic staff."

"Oh no, it's not," she fumed in reply. "Keep your hands to yourself in future – or else."

He just laughed away her protests and moved to let her pass but she was determined to stay out of his way as much as she could until he went back to school. She picked up a basket of food which Mrs Garside had left for her to give to Laura to help out over the holiday. As she was going out of the back door she heard someone behind her and thought Martin had followed her again, but when she turned to give him another piece of her mind, she saw it was Christopher.

"I'm glad I caught you Polly. I hope you have a lovely time with your sister and her husband." He held out a small gift wrapped in shiny paper and taking it, stuffed it into her coat pocket.

"Thank you Master Christopher, I don't know what to say. It's very good of you to think of me."

"I hope you like them," was all he said and he turned and waved as he went back up the stairs.

As she walked along Whitecross Street and crossed the road to Beck Hill, she wondered at how two brothers could be so different. Christopher was as pleasant as the day was long, but Martin had a streak of nastiness about him that she couldn't explain.

When she reached the small house she had called home for so long, she opened the back door and found Laura with her head in her hands at the kitchen table. When she heard Polly come in, she quickly wiped her eyes and stood up trying to smile but totally failing to conceal her misery.

Looking around her Polly noticed the fire wasn't lit in the grate and dirty dishes were still in the sink. Laura herself looked as if she hadn't combed her hair for a week and was so thin she looked as if she would blow away with one breath of wind.

"What's happened, Laura? Where's Sean?" As soon as she asked the question Laura's face crumpled again and she flopped on the chair again and began to sob.

"Come on, don't cry," Polly cajoled kindly, "I'll make a cup of tea shall I then you can tell me all about it. Look I've brought some food and some tea from Mrs Garside up at the house."

Laura looked at the basket of food and drew a ragged breath. "Sean's left me Polly. I don't know where he is. I've been to the police but they don't know where he is either. What shall I do without his wages? I've no money for coal and no food in for Christmas. I haven't eaten for days – where do you think he's gone Polly?"

"Come on, you know what he's like. He's probably with his mates somewhere or drunk in a ditch. He won't have left you, Laura," no-one else would have him, she thought unkindly, but instead she said. "Look, there's still time to go down to the coal yard on Fleetgate and get a couple of bags of slack. I've got my wages so we can maybe get some meat from Mr Simpson on the way back."

"How will we carry the coal Polly? Fleetgate's a long way from here."

"We'll nip down Butts Lane and then come back up Queens Avenue where we can call in to the butchers. I'll pop next door and ask if I can borrow young Billy's cart, we can drag the coal back up on that."

47

Laura visibly brightened at Polly's positive attitude and she went to fetch her coat and dragged a brush through her hair while she waited. Polly came back with the cart which consisted of a pair of old pram wheels topped with a wooden board, she also brought George Taylor with her who was going to help them.

Laura was so pleased to see George she almost cried again with happiness but after asking her how she was, he pulled the cart along a few steps in front of the sisters. It wasn't long before they had two bags of coal and some logs on the cart and Polly was pleased George had offered his assistance as it would have been too heavy for them.

"George would you be good enough to take the cart back for us and leave the coal outside the back door. We've got some more shopping to do before the shops shut and we don't want to drag you around with us unnecessarily." Polly asked, seeing that he seemed impatient to be finished. He seemed happy to do as she asked and said goodbye but promised to pop round on Christmas day to see how they were.

They called at the butchers and he had a scrawny chicken left which he let them have cheap, some off-cuts of bacon plus the bone and some pork dripping. Polly paid for it out of her wages and she could see Laura looking longingly in the pastry shop window so she bought them a cake each for a treat and some bread which was the last on the shelf. Polly squeezed it and it didn't seem too bad so she thought they could have some toast and dripping for their tea.

In no time at all they had bought their vegetables, again acquired as cheaply as possible just before Mr Small closed and they headed for home. They were both pleasantly surprised to find that George had used their spare key which they had left with Mrs Taylor for emergencies, and lit a fire for them in the kitchen and left the grate made up in the living room so all they needed was a match to warm the house up again.

Laura looked as if she was about to drop she was so hungry, so Polly sat her down and gave her some homemade soup which Mrs Garside had put into the basket and made some toast and dripping. It was easily warmed up once the fire was going and eventually Laura had some colour back in her cheeks again.

Later that evening as they sat by the fire in the sitting room, it felt like old times again, before their parents had died and before the fateful day Sean O'Connell entered their lives. Polly looked at her sister and decided she needed taking in hand.

"If Sean doesn't come back soon Laura, you're gonna have to get a job and he can go whistle. If he's not providing for you, how can he expect you to manage? What about going down to Hoppers and trying to get your old job back? They're always looking for experienced people and you were good at your job in the tin shop."

"Yes, I know Polly. I'll try them after Christmas and see if they'll have me back. I just can't rest not knowing where he is though. He never said anything about staying away – he just didn't come home."

"Well that's typical of him isn't it? Never a thought for anyone else, he just comes and goes as he pleases and expects you to be waiting for him. Do him good if you locked him out."

"I know you don't like him Polly, neither do I most of the time, but I wouldn't want anything to happen to him. I don't love him anymore, but if he's going to stay away I wish he'd just say so."

That night Polly and Laura shared the big bed that used to be her parents, and reminisced of Christmases past. They talked long into the night but gradually both became quiet and slept until Christmas morning dawned cold, clear and bright with the most perfect blue sky they had ever seen. It had been snowing during the night and the beck looked to be iced over. The first thing they did was exchange the small gifts they had bought for each other. In fact Laura hadn't been able to buy Polly anything but as she was good with a needle, she had redesigned their mother's dressing gown and altered it to fit Polly. It looked perfect on her and Polly was so pleased she danced around the room in it and refused to take it off. Polly had bought Laura some soap and scent from the Chemists and handed her a sock stuffed with a small orange, an apple and monkey nuts in their shells.

It wasn't much but it was all she could afford and after they had cooked and eaten their Christmas dinner which, Polly noted, would do for Boxing Day too and make a nice soup for Laura later in the week, they sat down and played some board games which they found at the bottom of the wardrobe in Laura's room. George Taylor came round with his brother Len and they brought a small bottle of sherry and port which they had bought from someone who worked on a boat which was in for a refit down at the boatyard. The girls had never touched alcohol before and found the sherry very sweet but after downing a couple each, they found it wasn't so bad after all.

They would have put the radio on and had a dance but the battery hadn't been charged up because Laura hadn't had the money to take it to the shop. Instead they played cards and had the happiest day they'd had for months. Polly could tell that George was still sweet on Laura, but he was the perfect gentleman and kept his distance, respecting that she was a married woman. Laura didn't know if she was pleased or not as she was badly in need of a strong pair of arms to comfort her and tell her everything would be alright again.

After they had left to go to the pub for last orders, the girls flopped on the sofa and giggled for no apparent reason.

"I think we're a bit tipsy," Polly slurred.

"I think you might be right," answered Laura and dissolved into fits of laughter once again.

At that moment Polly sat bolt upright and then dashed to her coat and felt around in the pocket for the little gift that Christopher had given her as she had left The Elms.

"What's up?" Laura asked, startled as Polly rang for the door.

"How could I forget?" she brought the little gift-wrapped box into the room and opened it very carefully. Inside the box on a piece of cotton wool was a beautiful pair of clip-on earrings in the shape of butterflies.

"Oh, aren't they beautiful?" Laura gasped as she saw them. "I think they must be set in gold, Polly."

By this time Polly was stood in front of the mirror which hung over the hearth, and was clipping on the tiny offerings. She stood back to admire them and showed them off to Laura.

"Who got you them?"

"They were from Christopher. He gave them to me as I left this morning." Her face was all smiles and it had nothing to do with the sherry she had drunk earlier.

"I think he must like you a lot, Polly, to give you a present like that. He hasn't known you five minutes. Do you think you ought to keep them?"

Polly's face fell and Laura felt really sorry she had spoiled the moment for her and tried to make amends.

"Listen to me. Course you should keep them, but only wear them for special occasions, eh?"

Polly smiled again and was satisfied that she could keep the little gift, but she took them off and put them back in their little box in case she lost them.

It was getting late by this time and so they made a cup of tea and ate some of Mrs Garside's Christmas cake before going to bed. Polly hid the little box with her mother's dresses where she could be certain Sean would never look.

The next day passed in a blur of activity as Polly helped to clean and tidy the house before she went back to The Elms and her duties. She was thankful that the family had been invited away for the New Year and she wouldn't have to contend with Martin and his wandering hands and then after that, the boys would be going back to school until Easter.

Chapter 7

At the time that Laura and Polly were enjoying their short Christmas holiday together, Sean O'Connell was in Dublin with his wife Katie and their four children. The fact that he was married already hadn't stopped him from proposing to Laura for one minute, thinking the matter would be safe from discovery considering the distance between the two women. He had sold the gold and silver pieces of jewellery that he had stolen from the better off people of Barton, finding dealers in Liverpool only too happy to trade with him. He turned up just before Christmas full of high spirits at his marital home surprising Katie with a slap on the behind and a twinkle in his eye.

Katie's reception was cool to say the least, but when he showed her the money he had brought with him, she warmed up considerably taking it from him and hiding it from prying eyes, in an old teapot she kept in a cupboard high up on the wall. After a few jugs of Guinness and a good Irish stew he was feeling considerably better than he had for a while and was full of plans for the future.

"Sean, will you be staying a while now you're home? The children have missed their daddy, haven't you?" she asked the four children, all staring warily at this man their mother told them was their father. They couldn't really remember him, the eldest one being only six, the youngest was two and hid behind the legs of the others, not sure what to make of this man who their mammy had welcomed into the house. Sean had been away for eighteen months, working on the roads in England so he told Katie, earning enough money to get them better accommodation and put good food on the table.

"I shall stay as long as I can but I have business to see to here first, then we shall see," was his non-committal reply.

"Now don't be getting yourself into trouble as soon as you come back, Sean O'Connell. You've to see your mother too, she's been asking after you for months."

"I'll go and see her tomorrow, but first I want to hear all about what you've been doing with yourself while I've been away."

"I've been looking after your children Sean, that's what I've been doing. The money you've been sending hasn't been enough and I've had to take in washing. Just look at my poor hands, red raw so they are, and they used to be such pretty hands too."

Sean took her hands and kissed them gently, smiling up into her face as he caught the smell of lye soap. Katie had always been his first and only love, they had married when he was sixteen and she fifteen and they had had their first baby nine months later. Unfortunately, that one and the following two were stillborn and Katie had begun to despair that she would ever carry full term babies, but then she had four in reasonable succession and all of them survived. She thought herself a lucky woman to have such a fine husband and family even though he did leave her for months at a time, he always came back with his pockets jingling with money. This time she wouldn't let him take it and waste it on drink, she would insist he get her a house with running water, she was so tired of pumping it into buckets in the communal yard and carrying it back into the house.

Over the next three weeks she dragged him to see a variety of houses at differing rents, and eventually he agreed to a cottage with two bedrooms and piped water in a more affluent part of the city. Katie was over the moon and immediately set to work scrubbing and cleaning until each of the four rooms shone like a new pin. It seemed to her that her husband had turned over a new leaf, perhaps his drinking and thieving days were over and they could start to build a new life together at last. The illusion didn't last long, two weeks later he was off again, back to England he said, to build more roads but the next time he came back, he would stay for good.

Katie didn't complain, she knew he would be back sometime, all she had to do was wait until he'd made his fortune and come back for her and the children, she just hoped that he hadn't left her expecting another baby, she would have to take washing in again when he'd gone, but for now she relished her new home and to the children he became a distant memory again.

■■■

Laura was in the kitchen when the backdoor opened and Sean walked in as large as life, ten weeks having passed since she had clapped eyes on him. Her reactions were mixed, she was pleased he wasn't dead as she had begun to suspect, but disappointed that he had picked that particular day to come back. George from next door had asked her to the pictures and she had agreed to go with him. She had got her old job back at Hoppers in the tin shop making chain guards for push bikes, and with Polly's help, she had managed to pay off most of her debts.

"You gave me the fright of my life. Where have you been, Sean – I thought you were dead?" she gasped in surprise.

"Looking for work, that's where I've been. Trying to find something that will pay better than grave digging, that's what I've been doing." He looked around the cosy kitchen and made a mental note of the new things that had appeared on the shelves and tables.

"I've got my job back at the factory and I've managed to pay off a few debts," she explained before he could ask. "Did you have any luck with finding work then? You know you've lost your job at the cemetery don't you?" She knew her voice sounded sharp but couldn't care less. She hoped he would leave her for good then she could apply for a divorce, although such things were frowned on and she would have to suffer nasty talk from all and sundry, but she didn't care and wanted rid of him.

"I haven't been in the house five minutes and you're nagging already. If you're that flush you can give me some money to go and get a drink with. I need to catch up with a few mates and see if there's any work going around here."

Just then there was a knock on the back door and Sean yanked it open. George stood there opened mouthed when he saw him.

"Good evening, George, and what can I do for you?" Sean was all smiles for the neighbours.

"Oh, er, nothing really, I just thought I'd check on Laura and see if she's alright. We didn't know when you'd be back," George mumbled lamely trying to look over Sean's shoulder to see Laura.

Sean stood back and gestured dramatically at Laura, "Well as you can see George, she's alright, so if you don't mind I want to speak to *my wife* in peace," and with that he slammed the door shut.

"So that's you're little game is it? Been playing around with the neighbours have you?" He came menacingly close to Laura and she shrunk back against the kitchen table.

"No, Sean, don't!" she pleaded as he raised his hand to smack her across the face but she managed to dodge the blow and ran to the other side of the kitchen.

"I said, give me some money – I'm going out!" he shouted and she dived for her purse and pushed five shillings across the table to him. It was all she had until pay day but it was worth it to get him out of the house. He grabbed the money and pushed it in his pocket, making a mental note to speak to George Taylor as soon as he could. Glaring at

55

Laura he kicked his bag of belongings under the table and stalked out without another word.

Laura breathed a sigh of relief when he had gone and sat down slowly trying to steady her trembling hands by reaching for the teapot to pour a cup for herself but she shook so much she gave up the attempt. Instead she put her head in her hands and wept until she had no more tears to cry. She was trapped in a loveless marriage with a contemptible, brute of a man and she didn't know how she would survive.

She heard a presence behind her and turned around to find George looking at her from the open door, not knowing whether to come in or go out. He had heard Sean leaving and thought he would go and see if Laura was still in one piece. As she stood up and moved slowly and hesitantly towards him, he opened his arms to her and she fell into his protective embrace, knowing in that moment that she loved him with all her heart. He let her cry while he held her gently and stroked her hair, making soothing sounds as if he was dealing with a child.

"Oh, George, what have I done? I've been such a fool marrying Sean. He's no good. He's violent and a thief. I just don't know what to do."

"Things have a way of sorting themselves out, Laura. Don't worry things will look better in the morning, you'll see. Now let me get you a drink to calm your nerves."

She nodded thankful he was taking charge. She had hoped that she had seen the last of Sean, although what she would have done then was anybody's guess. Somebody had told her that if he didn't come back within seven years, she could presume him dead and marry again. Whether it was true or not she didn't know but now she'd never find out.

She had just let George out of the back door when there was a heavy thumping on the front one. As she opened it she was met by some big men wearing flat caps and carrying long lengths of wood.

"We hear that husband of yours is back Laura. Can we come in and see him?" one of them said from the gloom.

"Who are you?" she asked, frightened and threatened by their manner. She tried to recall the man's voice who had spoken to her but couldn't.

"We're his er, colleagues Laura. We want to ask him what he's done with the money he owes us."

"He hasn't got any money, he took mine and went out." she answered honestly. "How do you know my name?"

One of them swore and spat into the beck. "Come on lads, we'll try the Sloop, he'll probably be in there."

Laura closed the front door on them, pressing herself against it and gasping in terror at what might happen to Sean if they used those lengths of wood on him. Yes, she hated him, but she didn't want to end up nursing an invalid for the rest of her life. As she was leaning against the door she felt it give and Sean almost flattened her as he rushed past her up the stairs.

"Quick, close the door woman," he hissed as he flew to the top landing.

Laura closed the door and bolted it and then went to check the back door was locked too. She found Sean sitting on the top step sweating and out of breath as if he'd run a good distance.

"Don't open the door to anyone – got that?" he asked.

"Alright, but who are they, Sean? What do they want?"

"How do I know?" he said irritably but she could tell he knew exactly what they wanted but he wasn't going to tell her.

The next day, and for three subsequent days, Sean never left the house except in the dead of night. Laura went to work as usual and pretended that all was well, until Polly came at the weekend for her usual visit. Unsuspectingly, she breezed in through the back door and approached Laura to give her a sisterly hug and almost dropped her things as she felt a large hand go round her mouth and she turned wide eyed with terror to find Sean behind her. As he let her go slowly, he warned her to say nothing of his presence and she nodded.

"What's going on? When did you get back?" she demanded, "why did you put the fear of God into me just then?"

"Someone's after him," Laura said despondently.

"Why, what've you been up to now," Polly directed her question to Sean.

"Nothing, just a misunderstanding but just you keep quiet about me being here."

Polly turned to Laura and said, "Are you still coming shopping?"

"Yes, I need to get some food for the weekend." She picked up her shopping bag and headed for the door with Polly close on her heels.

It wasn't until they were half way up the High Street that Laura let out a long breath.

"I'm so pleased to be out of that house Polly. He's driving me mad."

"When did he get back?"

Laura stopped at the corner of Hungate and Junction Square and sat on a bench waiting for Polly to sit so that she could explain. After Polly had sat down, Laura looked around to see if there was anyone about and then started to relate the story to her. When she had finished Polly whispered, "Do you think he's stolen their money and spent it?"

"Yes, no doubt about it. Why else would he be going out in the middle of the night? He's probably trying to pinch more stuff and then he'll sell it and pretend nothing's happened. I wish he'd stayed away Polly, I really do."

"Maybe he'll go away again when it's all sorted out," Polly added hopefully. Then on a brighter note she said, "Guess what? I've been promoted – I haven't had a chance to tell you but you know about the trouble with Nanny Jane, well the mistress caught her red handed giving baby Michael some stuff to make him sleep. After they came back at Christmas I told Lady Beauchamp about my suspicions like she asked me to, and she laid a trap for her and caught her with the bottle and spoon in her hand, just about to give it to him. Anyway, to cut a long story short, she's gone and good riddance. Nobody liked her, so I'm now the official nanny to Michael. I've got a whopping pay rise – £1 a week now, can you believe it? So if Sean decides to do a disappearing act again, I'll be able to help out a lot more."

"Polly, that's wonderful news. I'm so pleased for you. I just wish Sean would decide to leave once and for all, and then I could get on with my life. I feel like a prisoner in that house. He only lets me go out to work and then I have to go straight home. It's just as well you were coming today otherwise he might not have let me go shopping."

"That's stupid, you have to go out and buy food and you're hardly likely to tell anyone where he is, are you?"

Laura giggled, "I wish I could but I don't know who it is who's looking for him. George has seen him though but I've managed to persuade him not to say anything to anybody."

The rest of the afternoon passed happily as the sisters, always glad to be together, did their shopping and caught up on each other's news. The town was buzzing with shoppers and the early spring sunshine made a pleasant afternoon. When they got back to Beck Hill Sean was prowling around the house liked a caged bear, making a general nuisance of himself. Now that the nights were drawing out, it was later in the evening when he could go out and disappear to do whatever it was he did.

It was three weeks later on a Saturday night when things came to a head and he could stand his isolation no longer. The only time he went out was for a walk in the early hours when he could be sure that no-one was around. He took it into his head to go and meet up with his cronies starting at the Sloop Inn near the ropery. He needed a good pub crawl to see him right he thought.

Laura and Polly were alone and asleep in the house when they heard someone banging on the door. It was just getting light outside and when Laura opened the door she found Constable Clayton standing outside. Blinking into the early morning light she mumbled a sleepy, "Hello Constable, what's up?"

"Can I come in, Laura?" he asked seriously.

"Yes, of course," she stood back and let the man through and showed him into the kitchen where Polly had been sleeping, but now was filling the kettle. When Constable Clayton sat down, they both sat down with him at the rickety old table and waited for him to speak.

"I'm afraid I've got some bad news Laura. We've just pulled Sean out of Butts Drain, he's dead I'm afraid love. A workman found him this morning on his way to work."

Laura sat stunned for a moment and then looked at Polly who had put her hand over her mouth. Laura didn't know whether to laugh or cry, she was free at last. That was the first and only thought that came into her mind and she felt ashamed. No more Sean flaming O'Connell.

She heard Polly say, "Laura, are you alright?" and she nodded, still speechless. Constable Clayton stood up and went to the kettle which was whistling steadily on the range and poured some water over some tea leaves in the pot.

Laura suddenly found her voice and spoke quietly, "Thanks for coming to tell me Constable Clayton. I'm sorry but I don't know what to say. You know what sort of a man he was. Do you think I'm callous because I'm not sorry – not sorry at all? All I can think of is how wonderful it will be here without him."

She promptly burst into tears and Polly put her arms around her and hugged her close. The policeman put the cup of tea near her arm before saying, "Have a drink Laura, you must be in shock. I'm afraid you'll have to come and identify the body. Do you think you'll be up to it?"

Laura opened her eyes wide in horror and put her hand to her mouth, "Do I have to? Is he badly beaten?"

"No, Laura, he's not beaten at all. He apparently fell into the drain while he was drunk and he either hit his head or got stuck. We're not suspecting foul play."

"Oh, what a relief!" she exclaimed. "When do I have to come down to the station?"

"Later on today please. I'm afraid we have to get the pathologist to do a post mortem as it's an unexpected and sudden death, but you can come down before all that. Shall we say about ten o'clock?"

Polly nodded her understanding of the instructions as Laura was staring into space, alone with her thoughts. Suddenly Laura jumped up.

"Did he have a key in his pocket constable? A door key that is? He's been hiding stuff in the room that Polly used to have and he wouldn't let us go in."

"I don't know. I haven't checked the body. Someone else will have done that. Do you want me to force the door? It probably won't damage it much."

"I think you'd better constable. I don't want stolen stuff under this roof, that is, if it's still there."

They followed Constable Clayton up the stairs and stood back while he pushed against the door with his shoulder. It didn't take much effort for the lock to give as the door frame was almost rotten and they peered over the policeman's shoulder to see what Sean had been so secretive about. Immediately in front of them was the bed which Polly used to sleep in and apart from it being untidy there wasn't a great deal out of place. Polly stepped into the room and lifted the candlewick bedspread which hung over both sides of the metal-framed bed and looked underneath. Laura lay down on the floor and pulled out an old suitcase which she recognised as Sean's and clicked the clasps on both sides open. Inside were some bundles of cash, silver cigarette lighters and cases, jewellery, and other items obviously stolen from people in and around Barton.

Constable Clayton stood back and scratched his head in amazement at the variety of stolen goods before him. Without asking permission he went to the wardrobe and chest of drawers and found more things tucked away in them. Laura and Polly just stood and stared in amazement at the haul and wondered who he could have stolen them from.

"I'm going to have to ask you to make a statement about all this Laura," the policeman said solemnly and Laura's heart skipped a beat, "I know you didn't know what was going on but just for the records, we will have to hear how all this came to be here."

"But I don't know. I'm as much in the dark as you are. Me and Polly were told to stay out of here and we did because we didn't want to feel one of his backhanders if we could avoid it."

"I'll take what I can in the suitcase, but I'll have to report it down at the station and someone else will come and interview you. Now if you'll just go downstairs I'll make sure the door is secure until they come."

The girls looked at each other nervously and did as they were asked. Later, when he had gone, they sat in the kitchen and tried to come to terms with what had happened. It was still early when they heard a noise from the backyard and George came to the door and tapped gently. Laura let him in and his look of concern touched her as he asked what the police had been there for.

"It's Sean, George. He's dead," was all she could say and then she dissolved into tears again.

"I don't believe it. How did it happen, Polly?" George asked over Laura's weeping head.

"Fell into Butts drain apparently. There was still a lot of water in it from the floods last November. He fell and hit his head on something while he was drunk," Polly answered. "Do you want a cup of tea George?"

"No thanks, Polly. I'm off to work now but I'll call in later and see how you both are."

George disentangled himself from Laura and whispered a goodbye to her and went back next door to tell his family what had happened. Five minutes later Mrs Taylor came in and asked if she could do anything, but knowing what a brood she already had to cope with, Polly said they were alright. She knew the rest of the day would be a tiring one for Laura, but she would support her sister and decided to go and ask Lady Beauchamp for an extra day off to help Laura deal with it all.

Chapter 8

Although understanding and sympathetic regarding the circumstances of Laura's bereavement, Lady Beauchamp, said she could only give her one extra day off, and a few hours for the funeral whenever that was to be arranged. Polly had to be satisfied with that but at least she had until Monday morning to do what she could. Laura's experience at the police station had been difficult but at least she knew for sure that the body was Sean's. She was advised that once the post mortem was over and the coroner had called an inquest and delivered a verdict, then she could arrange to have Sean buried. There was also the question of the stolen goods to be sorted out.

Polly's first duty was to speak to the vicar on her sister's behalf, but when he visited the house he pointed out that as Sean had been a Catholic, they should speak to the local priest. Neither of the girls had had any prior contact with a minister from another faith, so the vicar kindly took it upon himself to inform the relevant man. They were glad that this responsibility was taken off their hands and so it was on Sunday afternoon, Father Joseph Riley knocked on the door and they invited him in.

"We didn't expect you so soon Father," Laura said trying to tidy cushions and clear away cups, "we only found out yesterday."

"I know child, but I thought I'd come and see you, as you'll be wanting to get the arrangements out of the way won't you." The priest's accent was a kind, lilting variety of Irish, unlike Sean's which had always had an edge. He smiled and sat down accepting a cup of tea and a slice of homemade cake that Polly had brought from the productive Mrs Garside.

"Yes but neither of us know where to start, so we will be more than glad of your help."

"Did Sean have any family?" Father Joseph asked and was surprised by the blank look on both their faces.

"He never spoke of anyone Father. He might have mentioned his mother but she lives in Dublin. Do you think we should try and trace her?"

"Well, I think I'd want to know if my child had died, wouldn't you?" he asked quietly.

"I'll have a look through his things Father, if that's alright Laura," Polly said and disappeared up the stairs.

Upstairs in the bedroom which Laura and Sean had shared, she opened the wardrobe and looked through boxes and envelopes, but found nothing relating to Sean. It was strange that he had lived in the house for a couple of years, and there was really nothing personal of his lying about the place. Finding nothing in the wardrobe, she looked under the bed and pulled out the bag that he had arrived with and probably used in his nefarious activities.

It was a large brown canvas hold-all and had a sturdy zipped pocket in one side. Drawing the zip back she found an envelope containing a picture of Sean standing between two women and four children. Looking on the back there was the date, only a few weeks ago, and an address scribbled in pencil.

Taking the envelope back downstairs she handed it to Laura. "Is this any good, Laura? Do you recognise any of the people here?"

Laura took the photograph and studied it closely. "I've never seen this before, where did you find it?"

"In the bag under your bed - look at the date on the back, it's quite recent."

Laura looked on the back and then at the front again, she couldn't explain who these people were and felt quite at a loss. She handed it to the priest who said, "I recognise the address, it's a street in Dublin that I know quite well. I should be able to speak to Father Patrick Donnelly of St Margaret's Church, in Dublin. He should know who these people are."

He looked at Laura and added, "Would you like me to do that Laura? Perhaps this is his mother, sister and her children and they should know about Sean shouldn't they?"

"Yes, Father, it would be best if you did it. I didn't know any of Sean's family. I didn't even know he had a sister. To tell you the truth, Father, we didn't even know he had been to Dublin recently. He told me he had been looking for work and had been away quite a few weeks. I was beginning to think he had left me."

Laura gulped and tears came to her eyes as she spoke. She felt so guilty about her feelings of relief that she could hardly speak to the priest. Father Joseph misunderstood her tears and patted her hand comfortingly.

"There, there, child, let it out. Grief is something we all have to deal with at some point in our lives, but you must have had your fair share with your mother and father being gone too."

His words, far from comforting her, made her worse. She lost control and sobbed while Polly tried to converse with the priest.

"How will you get in touch with the priest in Dublin Father? Will you write or can you telephone?"

"I'll try both. If one doesn't work then the other must. I will let you know what result I have but now I must be going to get ready for tonight's service. Thank you for your hospitality, and I'll see you soon."

Laura gathered her composure and stood to let him out of the front door, but he held out his hands saying, "No, my dear. You stay here and I'll see myself out. Thank you for your hospitality."

When the time came to go back to The Elms, Polly was looking forward to getting some normality back into her life. Laura said she would continue to go to work and try to pick up the pieces of her life while waiting for the inquest to be held.

It was only two weeks later after the post mortem results were available, and the coroner could hear all the evidence, that he returned a verdict of accidental death while the subject was under the influence of alcohol. Father Joseph returned and said he had written to Father Patrick in Dublin and was waiting for a reply. The telephones weren't reliable but as soon as he heard anything he would be back to see them and arrange for the interment of the body.

Polly was home one Saturday afternoon just after the verdict from the inquest when she answered a knock at the front door and opened it to find the vicar and the priest standing side by side looking quite solemn. After asking them in and getting them a cup of tea, she and Laura went into the sitting room to hear what they had to say.

"We've come with some disturbing news, Laura," said Reverend Cooper "but I'll leave it to Father Joseph to explain it to you."

Father Joseph coughed and leaned forward looking uncomfortable and fidgeted before he spoke.

"Laura, I've had a reply from Father Donnelly and it's taken a while because Sean's family had moved address and he hadn't known where to find them."

"Well, that's good news isn't it?" Laura said brightly.

"No, I'm afraid it isn't. They want Sean's body to be sent back to Dublin."

"Oh, I won't be able to afford to do that Father - I just haven't got the money for that kind of expense."

"We will do that for you, Laura – the Catholic Church looks after it's own you know," he gave a sidelong glance at the vicar before continuing, "but there's something else you should know." He fidgeted again and Polly wanted to hurry him up so interceded on her sister's behalf.

"You'd better spit it out, Father, what is it?" she said kindly.

"The photograph we saw showing the women with four children, er, one of them was his wife Katie and the children are his too. The other lady, as we guessed, is his mother."

Laura looked from one to the other, "But that can't be right Father. We were married over a year ago, in the Registry Office."

"Yes, I know Laura, but Sean committed bigamy when he married you. His wife was in Dublin waiting for him to come back with some money so they could get a better house and live as a family together."

Polly sat wide eyed listening to the conversation passing back and forth, "So all the time we were living here in misery with Sean O'Connell he was married to someone else?"

"Yes, I'm afraid so, Polly," said Reverend Cooper apologetically.

"But that's terrible. Laura lost a baby thanks to him beating her, and he took all our money and treated us like dirt."

Laura stood up and paced backwards and forwards across the room.

"What do I do now?" she asked.

"The best thing you can do my dear, is forget about this whole nasty business. He was obviously a bad man and the sooner we reunite him with his family the better," Father Joseph answered.

"Has his wife been told about me?" she asked

"No. Father Donnelly spared her that knowledge and we hope you will leave it that way, Laura. Although, I understand your feelings....."

His speech was interrupted by Laura starting to laugh hysterically and when she didn't stop after a minute or so, Polly had to shake her to make her stop.

"I'm sorry Polly," Laura gasped. "It's just so ironic. I've hated that man so much for so long, and all the time I wasn't married to him. I could have thrown him out and he couldn't have done a thing about it. What a fool I've been."

Father Joseph and the Reverend Cooper looked at each other in surprise at her words and feeling somewhat embarrassed, they stood up to leave. As they were going out of the door Laura said, "You can do what you like with Sean O'Connell, Father. Send him back to Dublin – they're welcome to him."

She slammed the door purposefully and went back into the sitting room where Polly was tidying away the dishes into the kitchen.

Laura studied her left hand and slowly took off her mother's wedding ring and placed it inside the sideboard drawer. Smiling to herself she closed the drawer and then turned to help Polly. There was an unspoken vow between them that they wouldn't mention his name again.

Life had begun again for Laura, and Polly was only too happy about it.

Chapter 9

Apart from the worsening situation in Europe and the political uncertainties, Polly and Laura settled into their lives once again. Laura was happily courting George Taylor, but was in no hurry to make it a permanent arrangement, and Polly was very happy at The Elms with the Beauchamp family.

Michael was growing fast and by the time war was declared in 1938 he was old enough to be educated and Polly was able to fulfil that role too. Her own schooling had been adequate for her to teach the little boy his ABC's and the rudiments of arithmetic and, for now, his parents were happy with his progress. Martin joined his father's old regiment and took up a commission at Sandhurst, while Christopher, that little bit younger, had chosen to enter the Royal Air Force when he left school.

Apart from the odd innuendo from Martin, Polly hadn't had any more trouble with him attempting to touch her, she mostly put this down to staying out of his way as much as possible, but also because he spent less and less time at home during the holidays. He had preferred to stay with one of his friends from boarding school who lived in London, where there was more to do than in the sleepy market town. Christopher was another kettle of fish as he always came home for the holidays and spent a great deal of time in Polly's company, so naturally she got to know him better than his brother. She was anxious when at 19 years old he joined the RAF but thought how handsome he looked in his blue uniform, but conceit was not part of his nature and he was still the Christopher he had always been. He was posted to the Central Flying School where he graduated with honours and earned his wings. His mother said she was so proud she could burst and his father shook his hand for so long Christopher thought it would drop off.

Martin on the other hand was at Sandhurst training to be an officer, but the difference between the two boys was pronounced when they returned home on leave together. Christopher was his usual jovial self but Martin was surly and arrogant. Polly disliked him more and more every time she saw him and still contrived to keep out of his way, but by this time he had lost interest in her and ignored her for the most part. By 1940 Martin had been posted abroad and his letters home were censored so no-one really knew where he was. Christopher on the other hand was based at RAF Scampton which was near Lincoln, not so far away, and he could return home during his leave, not that there was much time for that.

Another positive for Polly was that she had studied the way her employers spoke and had tried to emulate them. Her vocabulary had improved and her local accent was less pronounced.

One bright spring day in 1940 Polly decided to take Michael for a nature walk in Baysgarth Park, where they could identify the different leaves which had carpeted the grass last autumn and identify any new spring flowers which might be around. She was putting his coat on in the hallway when the front door opened and Christopher came in laden with his kit bag and limping quite badly.

"Oh, you made me jump Master Chris," Polly said with her eyes wide. Michael ran to his elder brother whom he idolised, and clung to him causing a shaft of pain to sear his left leg and a sharp intake of breath as agony creased his face.

"Oh, no Michael, be careful old man," Chris said as he held him away from his body and ruffled his hair. "I've got a bit of a gammy leg at the moment."

Michael was at once contrite and stood back as Polly went to help Christopher into the hallway and close the door behind him.

"What have you done Chris?" asked Polly, momentarily forgetting the Master pre-fix.

"Just a bit of an accident and torn some ligaments in my knee. The docs say it will be OK and I will be fighting fit again after a couple of months rest. Where's mum and dad?" he added before limping to the drawing room door. Martin and Christopher had been young boys when their mother had died, so Christopher naturally referred to his step-mother as his mother, Martin on the other hand had been slightly older, and sarcastically referred to her as step-mamma.

"Your father had to go to London and your mother went with him to do a bit of shopping in the West End."

"I should have let them know I was arriving, I suppose, but I didn't want to worry mum so I thought I would just turn up. Where are you going?" he said noticing she had her hat and coat on and Michael was struggling into his boots.

"We're just going to the park to see which trees are out in leaf and to see if Michael can identify them and any flowers. It's a bit of nature lesson. I don't suppose you're fit enough yet to join us are you?"

"No, not at the moment. I think I'll let Mrs Garside pamper me for a while." He smiled his lopsided grin which Polly thought made him look so handsome and her heart turned over.

"Will you tell us all about your bad leg when we come back, Chris?" piped up Michael.

"Yes, old man of course I will, but it's not a very heroic tale I'm afraid."

Michael looked at Polly with glee and started to pull her towards the door. "Come on, Polly, hurry up then we can get back and hear the story."

Polly laughed and allowed herself to be pulled to the front door.

"I think this is going to be the quickest nature lesson we've ever had" she laughed as he pulled the door closed behind them.

Trying to keep Michael's attention focussed on the lesson in hand turned out to be a losing battle for Polly. No sooner had they gone through the gates to the park than Michael decided he wanted to go home but mindful of her employer's instructions, Polly dragged him around for half an hour before relenting and heading home. He had picked up some fallen leaves from the previous autumn and she carried them in her gloved hand and with the other she held Michael tightly in case he ran out across the road without looking. There weren't very many motor vehicles around but horses and carts were just as dangerous she told him.

Arriving back at the house they entered by the kitchen door so that their muddy boots could be cleaned before he managed to trail mud onto the carpets upstairs. Mrs Gardside had a hot drink waiting for them both and Michael was insistent that he and Polly went up to the sitting room to be with Christopher. Polly knew her place and after depositing Michael with Christopher she made to withdraw to the kitchen again.

"Polly, why don't you bring your drink up here with Michael and I? You can hear all about the woeful tale of the knee straight from the horse's mouth."

Michael jumped about shouting, "Yes, Polly, come on, go and fetch your drink too."

"Well, if you're sure, Master Christopher, I'll be a couple of minutes." Turning and closing the door behind her, Polly couldn't help but smile to herself as she thought of spending time with Chris, as she thought of him in her secret moments. She was developing a crush on the young man even though she tried not to and frequently told herself off for having fanciful thoughts.

Once back in the sitting room with the fire burning half way up the chimney, she noticed that the day had turned darker and it had started to rain.

"Looks like we just made it in time, Michael," she said as she pulled the little boy closer to her for a hug. During her five years with the Beauchamp family she and Michael had grown very close, but the time was coming when she knew his parents would want to send him to a proper school for a decent education. When she thought of this time which no doubt would be coming soon, a cold hand gripped her heart and squeezed it tight, until she had to think of something else or she would surely cry.

Michael ran to the window and watched as large drops of rain crashed against the glass and the wind picked up, causing the smoke from the fire to swirl in the grate.

"Well, you know what they say about March winds, Polly. In like a lion and out like a lamb. So it won't be long before we get some nice April showers instead," Christopher smiled at her.

He had developed into a tall, broad shouldered young man and his hair had a habit of flopping over one eye when he spoke animatedly. Polly often imagined herself brushing it back for him and running her fingers through its silkiness. His open face invited confidences and his crooked smile made her weak at the knees.

"Polly, did you hear me?" Christopher had been speaking to her but she had been lost in her fantasy.

"Sorry, Master Christopher, what did you say?"

"Please don't call me Master while we are alone, Polly. It sounds so subservient and I hate it. Please call me Chris like everyone else."

"Alright, but only when we are on our own," she smiled back. "How long do you think you can stay at home?"

"Well, I've torn the ligaments pretty badly, so the doc says a couple of months. Can you put up with me for that length of time?"

"I think I can manage that," she said brightly, her mind trying desperately to wander off again and fantasise about what might be.

"Chris, Chris, tell us about your bad leg now" Michael interrupted.

Christopher went on then to describe how they had been playing football at the RAF base on a make-shift pitch. Unfortunately, after a bad tackle in which he had twisted his knee anyway, he had chased after a loose ball, which had been passed to him and promptly caught

72

his foot in a rabbit hole and sprawled headlong causing more damage to his knee than he had originally thought.

Michael was in stitches listening to his brother's description of how the accident happened and was hugely pleased that he would be staying at home to get better for a couple of months.

"Your parents will be pleased too. I know they worry about you," added Polly.

"Do you worry about me, Polly?" Christopher asked, suddenly serious.

Polly was flustered to say the least but managed to nod her head and smile at him, trying to convey her feelings through her eyes rather than words.

"I'm glad" he replied quietly, and reached over to touch her hand.

Polly felt as if his touch burned her skin and blushed so much she had to get up and walk to the window.

"Look, the sun's out again, Michael." When there was no reply she turned to see Michael had fallen asleep on the sofa and Christopher laughed, which seemed to break the spell between them. Any awkwardness she might have felt was erased by his laugh and she felt at ease again.

Just then Mrs Garside came in to collect Christopher's crockery and caught the easy atmosphere in the room. She looked from one to the other and sniffed her disapproval before asking Polly to help her clean away, thus conveying she should know better than to laugh and joke with her betters.

Polly at once went to help and Christopher understood that he must be careful how he handled his pursuit of Polly, if indeed that is what he intended, as it could lead to trouble for her. He must think carefully about how he felt about her and whether or not there might be a chance that she might like him as much.

When the door closed on the two women, Mrs Garside was immediate in her warning, "You should know your place, Polly, there will be no chance for you with him; his parents wouldn't allow it."

"I don't know what you're talking about," Polly retorted. "We were just laughing at Michael that's all."

"Well, that's as maybe, but no good will come of you and him. I know for a fact that his father wants him to court Betty Osgood. Her father's a good businessman and he wants the best for his sons."

Polly's heart felt like a lump of stone and her face went pale, but she managed to hide it from Mrs Garside by starting the washing up.

73

Betty Osgood was a beautiful girl and had been May Queen before the war. Polly didn't stand a chance of any kind of relationship with Christopher now. She wished she could go back to her room and was glad that it was Saturday the next day so she could go home to Laura. Laura would talk to her and help her see sense.

Since the war had started, Polly had been given two full days off per week, so early the next morning she took her small weekend case with her and was hoping to leave the house before Mrs Garside arrived, but as she opened the back door the two women almost collided as they both tried to get through the door together.

"My goodness, Polly, you're early today. Is there something special happening this weekend?" The older woman seemed to have forgotten their slight disagreement of the previous day and was as bright as always.

"Me and Laura are going to the Assembly Rooms tonight. The vicar has organised a dance and there will be a band too. I'm really looking forward to it."

"I remember the old tea dances we used to have in the Assembly Rooms," Mrs Garside reminisced. "We used to have some lovely times."

"Why don't you come tonight then?" Polly asked, trying to imagine a young Mrs Garside in the arms of a beau.

"Good heavens, no. My dancing days are well and truly over – but you and Laura have a lovely time."

"Thanks, Mrs Garside. By the way, Sir Giles and Lady Beauchamp arrived home late last night, and Michael was still asleep when I looked in on him, so you should have an hour or so before you are needed to cook breakfast."

"Alright, thanks Polly. See you on Monday."

Their goodbyes said, Polly closed the kitchen door and sighed with relief that she hadn't brought up the subject of Christopher anymore. She was hoping to tell Laura all about it when she saw her. The church clock told her it was barely 7.30am and she decided to go to Simkins's bakery to get a fresh loaf from Mary's dad before going home to Laura.

The bakery wasn't open for customers at that time but Polly knew Mr Simkins was always up early getting things ready for a busy Saturday in the shop. Mary would probably be there too, so Polly went around the back of the shop where the bakery stood, attached to the main building. It was hot in there and Polly was pleased to get warm as the March wind was still biting through her thin coat. Mary was pleased to see her friend and asked her father for five minutes off so that she could have a word with Polly. She made tea and they both sat at a small table at the back of the shop and they ate a cake each which had been baked the day before and therefore wouldn't have been sold in the shop as fresh. Mr Simkins sold all his left-over bread and cakes at half price and very rarely had to throw anything away.

Coming in from the bakery he squeezed another cup of tea out of the pot and leaned against the door listening to the two girls chatting. Polly felt that she ought to say something to him to bring him into the conversation, especially as she was drinking some of his tea, which rumour had it, was due to be rationed in July.

"How is business, Mr Simkins, with the rationing and that?" she asked.

Claude Simkins pulled a face as shrugged his shoulders before answering.

"Things are not too bad at the moment, Polly, but I think it's gonna get worse before it gets better. It's difficult to get butter already so I'm having to cut down on my baking. Even margarine is rationed now, and sugar is almost a thing of the past, but I'll try to keep going for as long as I can."

"I know it's hard to get now. Mrs Garside is always complaining about not being able to get any bacon unless she queues for it.

Mr Simkins drained his cup and left the two girls to chat, calling over his shoulder to Mary not to be too long.

"Are you going to the dance tonight, Polly?"

"Yes, me and Laura are going. Shall we see you there?"

"Yes, I'm meeting Meg Parkin. In fact, I'm going up to the farm this afternoon. Do you want to come? Laura can come too."

"I'd like that. I haven't seen Meg for ages and Laura used to go to school with her brother Richard. I'll ask her if she wants to go. What time are you going?"

"Dad says I can take the afternoon off, so I'll be going about 2 o'clock."

"We'll call for you then, shall we?"

Mary nodded and after briefly looking in her father's direction she stood up to start work again and Polly went into the shop to buy some bread to take home with her. Mr Simkins wrapped the still-warm bread in a couple of sheets of tissue-thin paper and waived aside Polly's offer of payment.

"No need, love. I know your ration book will be with Mrs Garside so don't worry. The inspectors won't miss one loaf of bread."

"If you're sure Mr Simkins, thanks very much."

Polly went out into the blustery wind once more and made her way home to Laura who still lived in the little house on Beck Hill, only to find her getting ready for work.

"Oh, Polly, thank goodness you've come early. I wanted to see you because I've been asked to work a few extra hours this morning. I hope you don't mind, but the money will come in useful."

"No, that's fine. I've brought some fresh bread from Mr Simkins; it's still warm." She pushed the loaf into Laura's hands, and as she held it tight she sniffed the yeasty smell.

"Mmm, lovely! We'll have some of that at dinner time."

"I'm going with Mary to see Meg Parker this afternoon at the farm. Do you want to come?"

Laura thought for a minute before saying, "Yes, alright. I've been feeling a bit low lately as George seems to have been away for ages. Goodness knows where he is, but I really miss him, Polly."

Thoughts of Christopher filled Polly's mind and she answered "Yes, I know what you mean. I want to talk to you later Laura. I need your advice on something."

"This sounds intriguing. I have to go now, but meet me from work and we can get some chips and have some of this lovely bread before we go call for Mary."

With that she was fled through the back door so as not to be late. Laura had moved from making bicycle parts to making shell casings at the Hoppers factory. All the women had their hair hidden in a turban headscarf to stop it from getting caught in the machinery as they turned the shell casings on a lathe. Not all accidents were prevented in this way, but the majority of women were very careful, as catching their hair in a lathe would scalp them in seconds.

The Hoppers factory still made bicycle parts and two of George's sisters worked assembling wheels, whilst another worked with Laura producing shell casings for bullets. Laura joined the three sisters on Queen's Avenue just before going into the factory. Nellie and Kitty went into one part of the factory to do a few hours overtime putting wheels together while Emma, known as Em or Emmie, joined Laura in the long section of the works making the shells. They all wore the unofficial uniform of a turban, apron and a swagger- coat. Almost all the men who worked there wore dark coats and caps with a white muffler round their necks. It was difficult to tell who was who as they all looked the same. Cycle production had gone up due to the large order from the Ministry of Defence for bikes for the armed forces and there was plenty of work around.

Polly wondered where the time had gone as in no time she was putting her coat on again to go to meet Laura from work. Her mouth was watering at the thought of chips and bread with a scraping of margarine washed down by a hot cup of tea. She arrived at the factory just as the work's hooter went. Within seconds hundreds of people were spilling out of the factory, all trying to get to the gates first. Polly stood on the other side of the road so that she wasn't lost in the stampede. Laura eventually saw her and wandered over. Nearly all the women walked in the same way and even though it was a windy March day, their coats were pushed aside by their arms as they put their hands behind their backs.

Polly and Laura walked arm in arm up King Street and crossed the road into George Street before joining the queue at the chip shop.

"Do you think there'll be any fish?" Laura asked, "I'm starving after working all morning."

"We can always ask, I suppose," Polly answered. "If not, we can have a fish cake each."

When they got to the counter Laura asked if there was any fish and to their joy they got a large piece of haddock which they intended to share and tuppence worth of chips. With their dinner neatly wrapped in newspaper they hurried back to the house and Polly lit the gas under the kettle for a hot cup of tea. Ten minutes later they sat down to their feast and Laura asked between mouthfuls, "What did you want to talk to me about, Polly?"

"It's about Christopher Beauchamp. I really like him, Laura, and after yesterday I think he likes me. Mrs Garside caught us laughing together and put me firmly in my place. She said his dad wants him to court Betty Osgood as her dad is a businessman. What do you think?"

Looking at her sister's earnest face, Laura tried to think of a way of letting her down gently, but in the end had to be blunt – for her own good.

"Well, I think Mrs Garside is probably right, Polly. I'm sure he does like you because you're a very likeable young lady, but I don't think there's a future there for you. Just think of the different backgrounds you have. He has led a really privileged life, and us, well we're from Beck Hill. You can't get more different."

"I know all that, but I can't help the way I feel." Polly's eyes started to fill up with tears and Laura leaned over to hold her hand.

"Try to forget him, Polly, before it gets out of hand. You still have to work there and if his parents get to know how you both feel, you'll get the sack. Try to think about the dance tonight and maybe you'll meet someone who will take your mind of Christopher."

Polly dried her eyes and sniffed into her handkerchief. "I know you're right, Laura, but it's so hard. He asked me if I missed him when he was away, and I told him I did. He said he was glad."

"Well, all young men like to think there's someone, somewhere, waiting for them to come home from the war. I don't suppose Christopher is any different."

Polly took a deep breath, took a long drink of her tea and finished her dinner. She decided she would take Laura's advice and enjoy her weekend with her friends and her sister. By the time they had finished the washing up and Laura had changed out of her work clothes, it was time to call for Mary.

Chapter 10

Richard Parkin had long since had a crush on Laura. Even at school he would find excuses to talk to her and carry her books, but now he was twenty five years old and looking for a wife. He had specific requirements for the job and listed them in his mind when meeting prospective girls. First of all they would need to be strong enough to work on a farm. Next she must be happy to have a large family, as many hands were needed to carry on the traditions his forefathers had lain down. He would put up with daughters of course, but sons were what he had in mind; six of them should be enough. As a farmer's son he wasn't necessarily required to join any of the armed forces, as his work was vital for the war effort too. Three of his brothers had decided to join the army together, so he was the only male left, apart from his father, to run the farm of thirty acres.

When Mary, Polly and Laura turned up for an afternoon visit with his sister, Margaret, known to her friends as Meg; he found that he hadn't lost any of his enthusiasm for Laura's company. She on the other hand, had definitely lost any she might have had for him. Their paths didn't cross very often, and it had been some years since she had seen him, but absence hadn't made her heart grow any fonder of him during this time, a fact that she didn't hesitate to convey as quickly as possible. Unfortunately, Richard had a very thick skin and didn't understand the subtleties of a hint.

The girls had entered the farmyard through the gate from Brigg Road and after negotiating two yapping border-collie dogs, they made it to the farmhouse door. The heat from the farm range hit them as they walked into the untidy porch where they took off their wellington boots. The large farmhouse table dominated the kitchen cum living room which had been cleared of the dinner time debris. Two sofas stood against adjoining walls, both of which were covered by loose covers and crocheted throws, and both had seen better days. Polly was unsure of whether to sit or stand as she suspected fleas lurked in the folds of the throws, but Meg was oblivious to her discomfort and insisted they all sat down. Tea was made and homemade scones placed before them with real butter to spread on them.

"These scones are delicious, Meg," Laura said.

"Gran made them. She should be coming through in a minute after her nap. As soon as she hears we have visitors she can't wait to see who it is," she laughed.

Meg's mother, Joyce, came in from the farmyard at that moment carrying a basket of eggs with her. She greeted the visitors and helped herself to a cup of tea and a scone. No sooner had she sat down than Meg's Gran decided to make an appearance so fresh tea was made and they all sat around the large table to catch up on the local gossip. Inevitably, the conversation turned to the dance at the Assembly Rooms that evening, and who would be wearing what.

"I remember the old days when we had real dances," piped up Gran. "It's all different now, and the music – if you can call it that – is so loud."

"How do you know, mother? You haven't been to any of the dances for years." commented Joyce.

"I've heard." The sulky retort came back instantly. Meg's grandma was famous for her droll sense of humour and caustic comments but she enjoyed being among the young people even though she seldom showed any pleasure in anything. Her curlers were hidden under a turban headscarf and tied at the top with two curlers poking out at the front.

"Well, we all intend to enjoy ourselves, don't we girls?" said Meg in defiance of her grandmother.

They chorused their agreement just as the door opened and in walked Richard.

"Enjoy yourselves doing what?" he asked, smiling in Laura's direction. "Hello, Laura. How are you keeping? I haven't seen you for ages, not since I heard about that so-called husband of yours." His tactless mention of Sean O'Connell made Laura blush and she stammered a non-committal answer.

"Go away, Richard. We're talking about the dance tonight and you said you weren't interested in going," Meg interjected, trying to take the tension out of the situation.

"I might be if Laura's going," he replied openly. This made Laura blush even more and Polly thought they might make their excuses and leave there and then, but Joyce told Meg to fetch her dress down and show it to the girls. The activity again moved the attention away from Laura who breathed a sigh of relief as she felt her colour returning to normal. She wished with all her heart that Richard would go out again, but felt his eyes on her back as she turned away from him.

Meg's dress was a celebration of yellow cotton, and she held it up for the rest of the girls to see.

"You'll look like a canary in that," scoffed Richard and stuffed another scone in his mouth.

"Don't take any notice of him," placated Joyce. "He's jealous because he isn't going to the dance."

"I am now," he said defiantly, and swung his body off his chair and stalked out into the farm yard to finish his duties there.

"It belonged to one of the land army girls," explained Meg. "She said I could have it as she didn't think the colour suited her."

"It's a lovely dress, Meg," said Polly touching the soft cotton material. "I think it will suit your dark hair and complexion really well."

Everyone agreed and Meg was suitably reassured.

"I think we'd better be off now, Polly," said Laura as she stood up and pointed at the clock on the mantelpiece.

"Oh, I didn't realise it was that time. We have to go and get ready now – shall we see you inside the Assembly Rooms?" Polly asked her friends.

"Yes, we'll wait for you near the cloakroom unless you're there first, and then you wait for us."

This agreed they made their way into the porch to put their wellingtons back on and huddle once more into their coats. Laura was very pleased that they didn't bump into Richard again before they left and Polly teased her mercilessly on the way home.

"Just think, if you get off with Richard and you marry him, his grandma will be related to you. Did you notice her knit one miss one teeth?"

"Stop being horrible, Polly. There is nothing on this earth that would tempt me into going out with Richard Parkin," but they laughed and nudged each other as they had done when they were children.

Back at the house they readied themselves as best they could, washing their hair and putting on what was left of the make-up Laura had collected before the war. They managed a scraping of lipstick out of an almost empty tube, which luckily enough matched Polly's pink shirt dress, and Laura wore a crushed velvet lilac creation she had altered from a pair of curtains she had found in her mother's box of clothes. Her eyes flashed attractively reflecting the lilac colour, and Polly thought how lovely she looked now that Sean O'Connell wasn't around to beat her down. They each drew a line down the back of their legs with an eyebrow pencil as nylons had become impossible to buy, thus creating the illusion of a seam. When they were satisfied with the results they set out to go to the Assembly Rooms. It was still windy outside so they huddled together and ran as best as they could along Burgate and into Queens Avenue to the hall which smelled musty with damp and age as they entered.

Meg and Mary were waiting for them at the cloakroom and having checked in their coats they went into the dance hall. A band was striking up a waltz as they entered and Polly took in the scene before her. A mixture of young men and women in uniform mingled with civilians, and chairs were lined up at the sides of the room. Most of the people were young but some older people had attended too, it was a church event after all and everyone was welcome. They had all made an effort to look nice and forget the drabness of wartime Britain. Just for one night at least they could pretend that this was an ordinary Saturday night. The colourful dresses of the ladies contrasted sharply with the khaki and blue uniforms. The girls went to get a soft drink from the counter at the top of the hall and then found seats with other girls Laura recognised from her work.

As the night wore on and bodies swayed to the music, Polly and Laura enjoyed chatting to the other girls and occasionally were asked up to dance. Polly loved to dance and accepted every invitation but Laura was quiet and was obviously missing George very much.

It was nearing half past ten when Richard Parkin lunged into the room, obviously the worse for wear with drink, and stumbled over to his sister at the far end of the room.

"I've come to take you home Meg, but first I want to dance with Laura." With that he grabbed Laura's arm and pulled her onto the floor. Laura was horrified and tried to wriggle free of his grip but he held her tight. She didn't want to make a scene so she stood woodenly on the floor while he dragged her round, standing on her toes and bumping into other dancers as they went. Laura constantly apologised to them until the music came to an end.

When the music stopped she left him where he stood and went to rejoin Meg and Polly. Meg grimaced at her and started to apologise for her brother's behaviour but Laura saw him weaving his way back through the crowd towards them and grabbed hold of Polly's hand and they ran towards the exit, taking a circuitous route in order to avoid him. A glance back told them that Meg was laying into her brother with her tongue and their escape would be easier now.

As they retrieved their coats from the cloakroom Polly felt a tap on her shoulder and turned to find a smiling Betty Osgood waiting to speak to her. "Hello, Polly. I haven't seen you for ages. How are you?" asked Betty.

Polly was taken off-guard and greeted her old friend warmly, "Hello, Betty. I'm very well thank you, and how are you?" Polly noticed with a pleasant shock that she was arm in arm with Ralph Taylor from next door.

"Good thanks. I've been hoping to talk to you for a while, but I've been busy with my dancing students. Did you know I was teaching dancing now?"

"Yes, someone mentioned it. How is it going?"

"Word is getting around and I'm quite busy now. We're thinking of putting on a display later in the year, maybe at the carnival if we have one this year. Do you fancy helping out?"

"Oh, I've never thought of doing anything like that, but I'll certainly consider it. Does this include Laura too?"

"Yes, of course. The more the merrier. Shall we get together sometime and talk about it? I can call round tomorrow if you like."

Laura had been listening to the conversation but with one eye on the door to the dance hall.

"Look, Polly. I don't want to interrupt you but Richard Parkin will probably be coming out soon and I'd rather not see him. Can we go?" she asked, nervously looking over her shoulder.

"Come round tomorrow afternoon, Betty. We can talk better then," Polly said.

They almost ran down the stairs and out of the building and didn't stop until they had reached home.

It was quite late by the time they were ready for bed and Laura was tired after working half the day, and the long walk up to the farm, so she went up straight away. Polly sat on in the sitting room in front of the banked-up fire and thought about Betty Osgood. Betty had had a charmed childhood being an only child but she wasn't spoilt. Her porcelain complexion and slim, toned, dancer's body was topped by lustrously thick black hair, falling almost to her waist when she let it down from its pins. She really liked her and she was always pleasant and never spiteful. Polly really wanted to dislike her because of Mrs Garside's revelation about Sir Giles' intentions, but found she couldn't and was really looking forward to seeing her friend the next day, not least of all because she wanted to hear how close Betty and Ralph really were. He was a tall, slim and quiet, young man who obviously adored Betty if his expression tonight was anything to go by when he looked at her.

After their exertions of the previous day the sisters had a long lie in and a leisurely lunch. Polly loved these days when it was just her and Laura and they could catch up with the gossip or listen to each other's news. As they were washing up the dishes she tried to draw Laura out on her thoughts on Ralph and Betty.

"Did you know that Ralph was seeing Betty Osgood, Laura," she asked innocently.

"No, not really. George has been gone for a few months now so I don't always know what's going on next door and Em hasn't mentioned it."

"Well, I was really surprised to see them together as she's from a wealthy family and he ...... isn't," she finished lamely.

"That just goes to show then, doesn't it? There's hope for you and Chris after all."

Polly took a deep breath and turned to her sister, "Do you really think so, Laura?" she let her breath go and smiled so wide Laura thought she would split in two.

"Of course I think so. It's only his parents that have big ideas for him and if Betty isn't bothered, then the road is clear for you. Now let's tidy up a bit as she'll be here soon."

They began in the sitting room and worked their way around the house, and within a couple of hours they had done the whole house. Polly worked like a Trojan to get the furniture polished while Laura took a dust pan and brushed the stairs. They had only just finished the bedrooms when Betty arrived and put her head round the back door and called to them.

Polly smiled her welcome and took her into the spotless sitting room while Laura made tea from their precious rations. They heard all about Betty's dance pupils and agreed to help her with costumes for them should the carnival go ahead that year, but all the time Polly was dying to ask about her budding relationship with Ralph Taylor. It wasn't until almost teatime and Betty got up to leave that she plucked up the courage to ask.

"Are you and Ralph courting then, Betty?" she blurted out.

"We will be if I get my way. We've known each other from school days and we've always liked each other," she answered conspiratorially.

"What's stopping you then?"

"Nothing really I suppose. It's just my mum and dad. They like Ralph but my dad wants me to marry somebody with business connections."

"Where have I heard that before?" said Laura sarcastically.

"What do you mean?" asked Betty.

"She means that Christopher Beauchamp has been told he has to ask you out" explained Polly.

"Christopher Beauchamp?" Betty sounded incredulous. "What's he got to do with anything?"

"I think his dad and yours have been getting to together and planning your futures," Polly said.

"Well, they can just go un-planning it then, can't they? I shall be having a few words with my dad when I get home."

"I'm so relieved, Betty. You see I really like Chris and I think he likes me, but his dad is a bit old fashioned and thinks he should marry into a wealthy family."

Betty smiled at Polly and reached out to hold her hand, "I'd hardly call us wealthy. You go for it, Polly. He could do a lot worse. Chris is a nice young man but my heart is set on Ralph. I hope you manage to grab some happiness, especially during these times."

When Betty had gone, Polly was on cloud nine and danced around the living room making Laura laugh at her antics. After their tea of sandwiches and a tin of fruit Laura had queued up for in the week, Polly had packed her bag and was about to start back to The Elms, when Meg puffed her way in through the back door.

"Hello, sorry to be so late but I've been sent on an errand by my mam. She says to tell you, Laura, that she's sorry for Richard making a nuisance of himself last night, and to give you these eggs."

She handed over a brown paper bag with two fresh eggs nestling inside, a rare treat in wartime. They were making do with powdered egg out of a tin, and it tasted vile.

Laura took the eggs and smiled at Meg. "Thanks, Meg, and tell your mam thanks too. These will make a lovely breakfast in the morning. Pity you're going back to the Elms, Polly."

Polly raised her eyes heavenward, "You never know, maybe Mrs Garside has collected a few from the bantams in the garden and I might be able to grab one before anyone sees them. Sorry I can't stay Meg, but I've got to get back. We'll go dancing another week shall we?"

"Yes, please. Hopefully we can get away without Richard finding out. He's really got it bad for you, Laura."

Polly left them talking in the kitchen and made her way back to the Elms to find it in uproar.

Chapter 11

Immediately she set foot over the back door threshold she found Mrs Garside in tears at the kitchen table.

"What on earth is the matter? It's not bad news is it?" Polly's face was ashen as she asked the question.

"Well, nobody's died if that's what you mean," Mrs Garside wept into her handkerchief.

"It can't be that bad then can it?" Polly tried to cheer her up and get the full story out of her. Mrs Garside hiccupped and sniffed into her handkerchief before starting to tell Polly that the Mistress was leaving. Polly looked amazed as at that moment Lady Beauchamp, never a frequent visitor to the kitchen, came down the stairs saying,

"Ah, Polly, I'm so glad you've arrived. Come upstairs with me would you and I'll explain what is going on."

Polly looked from Mrs Garside to her mistress and then back again before Mrs Garside nudged her off her chair and encouraged her with a smile.

"I'll be alright, love. Go with the Mistress."

Polly followed with her heart in her mouth wondering what on earth could be happening but the Mistress looked just the same as usual, so it couldn't be anything really bad, she thought. When they reached the hallway she was surprised to see half filled tea chests strewn around Mr Harrison was looking glum as well as out of breath as he wrapped ornaments and vases in newspaper and laid them gently in the tea chests. Before she got the chance to ask any questions she was ushered into the sitting room where Christopher sat with Michael on his knee. Michael immediately jumped up and launched himself at Polly blurting out the secret.

"Polly, we're going to Canada, and you can come too. Won't that be just wonderful?"

Polly stood stunned looking for answers but Christopher just shrugged his shoulders and looked towards his mother.

"Sit down, Polly, let me explain," Lady Beauchamp indicated an armchair and Polly thankfully sank into its plush comfort. "Michael shouldn't have told you like that before I had chance to give you the full story," she gave Michael one of her looks and he retreated back to Christopher's knee looking sorry for himself.

Lady Beauchamp then launched into her explanation. "You see, Polly, my sister lives in Canada and she has suggested that Michael and I, and you of course, if you want to that is, go to Canada for the duration of the war. Sir Giles is to lead a team of people in some project that he can't discuss, but it means he will be in London most of the time and he would feel safer if we took up the offer and went to Canada. What do you think? Would you like to come?"

Polly stammered, "Well, er, I don't know. This is all very sudden and I can't decide without talking to Laura." She looked over at Christopher but he looked away so that she couldn't read his face.

"Yes, well of course, we have rather sprung this upon you and you must feel able to say no, but there is a place for you if you want to come. In the meantime, I mean to pack up all the things which are breakable and store them in the cellar. My husband has offered half the house as a hospital for convalescing servicemen, so in that way there will be a home for Christopher and Martin when they come back on leave."

Polly was still shaken by the sudden events and Christopher took pity on her. "Why don't you let Polly go back to Mrs Garside and discuss this with her. She;ll need time to come to terms with all this. In fact, I still need time to come to terms with it."

"Yes, of course. Off you go then, Polly, and have a think. We'll talk about it later."

Polly was dismissed, she knew it, but found it difficult to get up from the chair. Her heart was beating twenty to the dozen and her strength seemed to have disserted her.

Christopher pushed Michael off his knee and went to put his arms around Polly to lift from the chair, but even in her bemused frame of mind she knew he would hurt his knee further if he put too much weight on it.

"I'll be alright, Chris," she said, unthinking that his mother was around to hear the informal way she spoke to him. "I'll just need a minute to gather myself and I'll go."

Lady Beauchamp didn't seem to have noticed her slip, and smiled at her, "You take your time, Polly. I have rather sprung this on you, haven't I?" She then caught sight of Harrison struggling to move a tea chest and went out of the room to see what she could do. Polly dared to look at Christopher's face but she couldn't read what was going on there. He stood up and walked to the window, speaking over his shoulder.

"I know. It was a shock for me too. They were full of it when they came back from London on Friday night." He ran his fingers through his hair which needed cutting, Polly thought, as she watched him.

"When are they thinking of going, Chris?" she asked almost reluctantly.

"As soon as possible it would seem. Father is due to take up his post a week on Monday so there is nothing to keep her here after that."

She stood up then and joined him at the window, daring to touch his arm as she stood next to him.

"Chris. I'm not going. I've decided. I can't leave Laura and I can't leave you. Not now."

Christopher leaned closer and pressed her hand with his own whispering, "I'm glad."

She left him then and went back down the stairs to the kitchen, where she was pleased to find Mrs Garside had pulled herself together enough to start making cocoa for Michael's bedtime drink. "Amy's gone and enlisted in a factory in Sheffield of all places, making ammunition - and now this. What's going to become of us Polly?"

"I don't know, Mrs Garside, but don't worry I'll help out when I can."

As it happened the big move didn't happen until nearly a month later. Everything that could be moved down to the cellar or up into the rooms occupied by Christopher and Martin was moved under the watchful eye of Mr Harrison. Sir Giles organised an army of men employed by Betty's father in his carting business to help with the process, so it was all done efficiently in the end.

Christopher's knee had healed with rest and light exercise so he intended going back to Scampton at the beginning of June. The worst part of the whole thing for Polly was saying goodbye to Michael. She had looked after him for five years and it was like parting with one of her own. Of course, she tried not to show it as she didn't want to upset him, but in the end she hugged him until they both cried. Lady Beauchamp was none too pleased about having a wailing youngster on her hands, but Christopher cheered him up with stories of the train he would be going on, and of course the aeroplane. After more tearful farewells Polly went up to her attic room and threw herself on her bed to give vent to the emotions she had tried to keep in check for weeks. She would be leaving once the house had been given a thorough spring clean.

Michael and his mother had been gone for a week or so when it was announced to the general public that the British forces were under sustained attack at a place in France called Dunkirk where an evacuation had been in progress for a few days, but things were now desperate. Anyone with a privately owned boat was asked to help and Christopher announced to Polly just as she arrived one day, that his father had a small engine-powered boat moored at Far Ings, a little way down the Humber. Not just that, he said he was going to help get the soldiers off the beaches himself. She was horrified to think of him making the journey alone and insisted that she would go with him.

Together they made their way down to the Point from where other people were leaving, and Christopher managed to get someone to drop them at their boat before joining the small flotilla, all of which were heading for France. Polly had only ever been on the ferry between New Holland and Hull so knew nothing of small boats, which was probably a blessing, as she was violently sick on the way out of the Humber estuary and into the North Sea. Although very embarrassed initially she began to get used to the pitch and toss as Christopher handled the small boat with great skill and her green pallor gradually faded. To her relief there was a small cabin which would probably fit four people, maybe five at a push, and there was room on deck for others. Mentally, she tried not to think of what was to come and concentrate on the job in hand. The journey was long and she was thankful that the boat had been well-stocked with basic supplies, including petrol, although there was also a small sail that could be erected if necessary. Her job was to make hot drinks and keep Christopher well supplied with these, but later he told her to go down to the cabin and get a little sleep if she could.

Between them they managed to navigate mainly by following the other boats which were heading in the same direction, but it was the noise which alerted them to the fact that they were near the coast of France. Eventually Christopher shouted to her to come up on deck. The sight that met her eyes was unbelievable as line after line of soldiers were wading out to whatever boat or ship was available, some holding their guns over their heads, others bandaged, some being held by their colleagues or medics in an effort to get them to safety. All the time this was going on, German aircraft were strafing the lines of men but a great cheer rang out when British aircraft joined in the battle and chased them off to fight them in the skies above.

Christopher and Polly were too busy to think about their own safety and hauled ten men aboard the little boat before turning round and setting off for the nearest English port. She was kept busy trying to make tea on the small stove for all the soaking wet men they had hauled aboard, and all were grateful for her efforts. Now and again bullets would come close to them, but thankfully and with many prayers offered, none hit them directly. The explosions were deafening and everyone ducked as a shell landed in the water about six feet away. Plumes of water drenched the men on the deck. One of the young men she offered a drink to, had been hit in the shoulder and was almost delirious with the pain. She looked around for a medical kit and found one under one of the seats. Without thinking she cut away the man's shirt and washed the wound. She saw that the bullet had gone straight through, and blood was pumping heavily onto the makeshift bandage someone had fashioned for him. The medical kit was basic and contained a box of pain killers, a couple of bandages, a pair of scissors and some iodine. In an effort to stop the blood flow she packed the wound with one of the bandages, but it was when she dabbed iodine around it that he fainted. This gave her the chance to wrap the other bandage around his shoulder and arm to keep the first one in place.

"That's a neat job you've done there, love," commented one of the medics they had brought on-board. "Are you a nurse?"

"No, I've never had to do anything like this before, it was instinct I suppose."

"Well, maybe you've found your calling then. We need people who don't faint at the sight of blood to help in the hospitals. You should think about training to be a nurse."

"Well, I don't know about that, but I'll certainly think about it."

Polly moved away to help the others and then piled dry blankets that she found also under the seats, on top of the now semi-conscious young man she had bandaged up. She gave him some pain killers from the box and looked around at the other men below deck and judged that they could cope without her for a while and returned to Christopher on deck.

"I hear you're a bit of a Florence Nightingale, Polly," he said smiling his crooked smile and making her heart turn over.

"No, not really, I've never thought of being a nurse but I will have to think of something else to do now that Michael's gone."

91

There was a roar above them as planes swept across the Channel and dog fights began in earnest in the skies. The men on the deck looked hollow-eyed and exhausted as Polly handed out the last of the hot drinks. Occasionally, there was a cheer when a British plane brought down a German one, but all Polly could think of was that even a German pilot had a family somewhere.

Christopher indicated a box at his feet built into the side of the boat and inside was a small bottle of rum which she immediately poured into the drinks which brought a glimmer of a smile to the men's faces.

"Thanks love, you're an angel," was muttered at her more than once from frozen lips and Polly felt such compassion for them she wished they could have rescued them all.

They followed the other small boats laden with their human cargo into Dover harbour, accompanied by a huge cheer from the men as they sighted the white cliffs, and found that medical posts had been set up along the front to help the injured men, and for those who weren't injured there were stations where they could report their safety and be transferred back to their units. Trains had been laid on to transport the able bodied and the badly wounded, the latter being sent to the town's Buckland Hospital. It was organised chaos as people were pushed and shoved from one place to the next but Polly and Christopher managed to off-load their men into the waiting hands of nurses and doctors. As a stretcher was brought aboard to take away the man with the wounded shoulder Polly went down into the cabin with them to help. He was conscious by now but in a great deal of pain. His ashen complexion and trembling lips touched her heart and she judged him to be about eighteen years old. He was lifted as gently as the confined space allowed and he grabbed her hand as they passed her. She looked at him and smiled saying, "You'll be fine now, you're back in England the doctors will soon have you patched up."

"What's your name?" he gasped

"Polly, what's yours?"

"Jim, Jim Carter," he smiled a twisted, pain filled smile as they took him on deck and then onto the quayside to be attended to.

"Looks like you have another admirer," Christopher came up behind her and put his arm around her shoulders. She turned into his embrace and finally her pent-up emotions found release in his arms.

Christopher let her cry for a while, and then tipped her chin up so that he could see into her watery, red eyes.

92

"I know you don't want to hear this, Polly, but do you feel up to going back and getting some more of our lads out of that hell hole? We will have to re-stock with supplies, especially fuel, but I bet the army or navy lads would let us have something to take with us."

The last thing Polly wanted to do was to go back out there but she knew he would go with or without her so she nodded wearily and dried her eyes. The decision made, Christopher told her to go and lie down for a while in the cabin and he would search out some provisions.

"But .... what about you, Chris? You must be exhausted too. Why don't you have a rest?"

"I'm OK. I haven't been able to do anything but rest for the last few months so now I have a chance to do something before going back to my squadron."

She knew it would be useless to argue so she went down to the cabin and lay down under some of the blankets the men had used while Christopher went off to find what he needed. Of course, there was the usual red tape, forms to be filled in etc, and by the time he arrived back it was almost dark. He was told by officials that he would have to move his boat out of the harbour as there were so many others to take his place. With great difficulty he manoeuvred the little boat out of the harbour and found a mooring some way off to allow others to off-load their cargo. They decided to spend the night in the boat and then go back again to rescue as many of the men as they could.

At daybreak they were woken by hooters and engines; there were shouts and yells as sails were hoisted and trimmed, so after a brief splash of water and for Polly, a very embarrassing encounter with a bucket, they were soon on their way once more. Again, following other boats and ships they made their way over the Channel. The scenes of men floundering in the water and being taken from the beaches by the smaller boats would have been spectacular had it not been for the reality of the situation. Christopher pulled in as close as he dared to the beach and one after another the men were helped on-board. Again, they took more than they should have, but there were still hundreds of men waiting to be rescued. It was an ordeal to have to pull away, but thankfully there were other boats pulling alongside to take their share too. They had moved away by about three hundred yards, when shells fired by the coastal batteries began exploding in their vicinity. The sound of whistling shells and screams as they found their target was horrific and Christopher re-doubled his efforts to make

93

a break for the English coast. Polly had just come up to see what she could do for the men on the deck when directly ahead of them a small tug took a direct hit. Men were thrown into the water again, most of them beyond help, but Christopher slowed down to see if there were any survivors. The men on deck helped to identify anybody who might still be breathing and pulled them on-board. Others were beyond help and were pushed back into the water. The little boat was so heavily laden Christopher was worried it might capsize.

Polly moved gingerly along the new intake and saw one young man in an army uniform lying almost face down sandwiched between two others who were now struggling to sit up. She tried to turn the man over to see if she might be able to help him but he put his arms over his head and assumed a foetal position. His hands were badly burned from the explosion and she looked at his colleagues for any help they might be able to give.

"He's a bit shell-shocked, this is the second time he has been blown up today, two other boats he's been on have sunk," came an explanation from someone nearby. "I hope its third time lucky then," someone joined in sarcastically.

Polly knelt down beside the young serviceman and gently tried to calm his nerves and pull his arms away from his head. She noticed his misshapen hands were black and red where burning oil had stuck to them. Christopher was too engrossed in trying to avoid obstacles to take much notice of what was going on. As the cacophony of sound died away the young man became more coherent and he gradually removed his arms and tried to sit up, but his hands were so bad he had trouble using them. As Polly reached out to help him their eyes met for the first time and recognition was instantaneous and mutual.

"Martin," she exclaimed.

"Polly, is that you?" he asked incredulously.

"Yes, and Chris is here too. This is your father's boat."

He tried to laugh but the pain was too much and his mouth turned down in a grimace. She turned around to look at Chris but he was busily engrossed in a conversation with a sailor to take any notice of what she was doing. Standing up she went over to him to get his attention. He smiled at her as she pointed over to where Martin lay in agony with his hands, but his smile disappeared in a flash when he saw who it was, even through the grease and grime stuck to his brother's face, he knew who it was. The sailor was immediately thrust in front of the wheel and was ordered to steer a course for Dover, while Chris jumped down to go to his brother.

"Well, this is a turn up for the books, old chap. I never expected to meet you like this. Let me look at your hands."

With infinite care Chris held Martin's hands in his own and shouted to Polly to get something to bandage them with.

"I can't, Chris, everything is used up on the men who are bleeding down in the cabin. The only thing I have is my petticoat, but it's hardly sterile."

"That will have to do. Go and find somewhere to take it off and I will tear it up for you. Is there anything else we can put on his burns?"

Polly wasn't convinced there was anything, but said she would go and have a look. Putting modesty aside she found a spot where she could take off her petticoat, which happily for her was only a half one held by elastic at her waist, and then went in search of the precious medical kit to see what was left, leaving Chris to try and tear the cotton into as many strips as he could. Finding the medical kit, she tore the lid open and found some petroleum jelly and some aspirin and ran back up on deck where Chris was tearing her petticoat into shreds. With great care she began to spread the jelly onto the burned hands but Martin was in agony and cried out all the time for her to stop. Chris tried to soothe him but to no avail so gave him the last of the aspirin. It didn't have much effect on the pain but it did calm him enough to allow the bandaging to carry on. Polly didn't know how to do it expertly but wrapped each finger individually after a liberal smearing of the jelly, and finally his hands. His fingers were bent over like claws and he was sweating liberally with the pain.

Hearing a shout from the sailor they looked up and saw the white cliffs of Dover on the horizon and realised that they had made it back in one piece again, but she doubted that there would be a third trip. An hour or so later they were again disgorging their human load to waiting ambulances and trains. Christopher looked exhausted and almost as hollow eyed as the soldiers themselves, but insisted they must accompany his brother until he was firmly stopped by army personnel who explained that if they took up room in the train that would leave less room for the wounded. With promises to visit him as soon as possible, Christopher found a telephone box and called his father to give him the news of Martin's rescue. Sir Giles promised he would make sure Martin had the best of care and noting the fatigue in his younger son's voice, ordered him to take himself and Polly home.

It was much later that they learned that between 26th May and 4th June 338,000 troops had been rescued from Dunkirk, with over 200,000 of them passing through Dover. They were proud to have been one of the 'little ships' which had helped to bring the soldiers home.

Chapter 12

Polly had been away for five days by the time they arrived back in Barton and although she was emotionally elated, she was physically exhausted and Christopher convinced her to go home to Laura. She was reluctant to leave him after being with him for such a long stretch of time but he was fully fit now and told her he was leaving Barton the next day to rejoin his squadron.

"Take care, Polly. Thanks for coming with me. You were so brave and I couldn't have coped without you. I'll really miss you."

"You take care too, Chris. I'll miss you too."

After saying their goodbyes, he gave her a long hug and a peck on the cheek and they promised to write to each other. Christopher left her at the corner of Whitecross Street and she made her way back to the house on Beck Hill.

"And where do you think you've been, young lady?" Laura asked as soon as she walked in through the door.

"Have you missed me then?" Polly answered cheekily.

"I've been worried sick our Polly. I went up to the house and they told me that you had gone off somewhere with Chris and nobody knew where. Mr Henderson thought you'd gone for a boat trip or something. I thought you'd drowned."

"Not exactly a boat trip, but there was a boat involved. Sit down and I'll tell you about it, but first of all put the kettle on and make a cup of tea. I'm parched."

During the next half hour Laura heard the story of her little sister's adventures and was horrified to hear that she had done the trip to Dunkirk twice. When she thought of the danger involved she closed her eyes and thanked God for her safe return. Her little sister meant the world to her and the idea of her putting herself in danger like that made her angry and proud at the same time. She heard about Martin's burns and expressed her sorrow and by the time Polly had finished her story, Laura was weeping into her handkerchief and Polly was laughing and crying at the same time.

"Oooh, our Polly, what am I going to do with you? Fancy going off like that without telling me, you could have been killed, both of you."

"It was done on the spur of the moment. If I'd thought about it, I don't think I would have done it, but I'm glad I did. It made me realise that I can do something useful after all in this awful war. Laura I'm going to go and work in a hospital, looking after the wounded. In fact, The Elms is being turned into a convalescent home for servicemen and I'm going to see what's needed to be able to work there."

Laura's face was a picture of disbelief and her emotions were written all over her face. Polly could see her struggle with the idea at first but then Laura relaxed and reached over to her little sister and hugged her for the first time since she had walked back in.

"Well, I think that's a wonderful idea, Polly. I'm sure they'll be lucky to have you there."

Polly smiled her thanks and looked around the kitchen for the first time to see boxes some of them half packed, stood in a cluster at the back of the door.

"What's going on here then?" she asked, indicating the boxes.

"I've got news for you too, Polly. I've agreed to marry George by special licence next Saturday, and we are moving to Chapel Lane. He doesn't want us to be too close to his mum and dad when we're married. He's renting us a house with three bedrooms."

Now it was Polly's turn to be shocked. "When did all this happen?" she asked and stared open-mouthed at her sister.

"Last night. He came back with a twenty four hour pass and popped the question. I had decided to accept weeks ago as I knew he was going to ask me again but I was surprised when he turned up on the doorstep. So you'll have to see if you have enough coupons for a new dress, Polly, as you're the only bridesmaid."

"But you can't leave me here on my own. What will I do without you?"

"By the sounds of it you'll be working and living at The Elms most of the time anyway, and if you don't want to stay here on your day off, then you can come up to Chapel Lane and stay with me there. There will be loads of space for you. We can either rent out this house or close it up until after the war and decide what to do with it then. What do you think?"

Polly sat for a moment and realised that she hadn't congratulated Laura on her forthcoming wedding and had thought only of herself.

"Of course, Laura, what am I thinking? Congratulations and I would be happy to be your bridesmaid. How exciting, you getting married to George at last. I know you are made for each other and he'll make you really happy."

"Thanks, love. Just imagine, no more newts crawling up the passage from the Beck. You know you always hated them."

Polly shuddered. "Yes, I shan't be sorry to see the back of *them* for a while. It's a good idea to rent or shut it up, which do you think we should do?" All of a sudden her eyes felt heavy and she couldn't stop yawning so Laura ordered her to bed to recover from her ordeal and said they would talk later and make plans for the future.

Polly was so pleased to sink into her soft, downy mattress that she fell into a deep sleep instantly.

It took her a couple of days to pull herself together after her ordeal at Dunkirk and gradually people became aware of what she had done. Some of the girls who Laura worked with were jealous and showed their spite by suggesting that Polly and Christopher were up to no good on the boat and they never went to Dunkirk at all. Laura was furious with them and gave them a tongue lashing they wouldn't recover from quickly. Others were genuinely delighted to hear that someone they knew, and a woman at that, was able to 'do their bit' in such a positive way. Polly was amazed when people came up to her in the street and congratulated her and wanted to hear the story from her own lips. To start with there were a few girls who nudged each other as she passed them in the street and whispered behind her back but she found that ignoring them was the best course of action. She was a little embarrassed but the news became a three day wonder and eventually it was forgotten in the day to day survival of wartime Britain.

Laura and George's wedding went off without a hitch and the two families pooled resources to put on a nice spread. Mrs Garside made a sponge cake for them but there was no icing sugar available, so they made do without. The eggs for the cake were donated by Meg's mother and they were both invited to the reception to toast the happy couple. Laura was pleased that Richard hadn't asked if he could attend but Meg seemed to think he had got over his crush at last. He now had his eye on one of the land girls. The reception was held at the house in Chapel Lane as it was bigger than Mr & Mrs Taylor's house and the furniture that had once been in the old place on Beck Hill now graced the living room and separate dining room of the new one. Children ran up and downstairs going from room to room and exclaiming at the size of the house.

"Is this just for you and our George?" asked Marie, now a lanky twelve year old, but showing signs of a natural beauty yet to be born.

"No, Polly's going to live here while George is away in the army," Laura answered.

"Will I be able to come and stay?" she asked cheekily.

"I don't see why not, we'll have to see what your mam and dad say."

Immediately Marie raced out of the door to ask Mr & Mrs Taylor if she could stay the night, not understanding that George and Laura wanted to be alone on their only night together as he had to be back at camp the following evening.

Laura laughed when she saw Marie's crestfallen face when it was explained to her, but cheered her up by telling her that she would be the first to be invited when she had furnished the bedroom properly.

The neighbours, Ivy Turgoose and her mother Mavis, were casting an interested eye over the furniture that Laura had brought with her and being a small community, the Taylors were acquainted with virtually everybody in the town, so were quite at home with George and Laura's new neighbours. Polly collected some plates and glasses from the guests and took them into the kitchen where she was joined by Mavis Turgoose, a woman of around sixty three years with no teeth of her own, but who had managed to suck her way through a large amount of potted meat sandwiches.

"Is there any of that jelly left, Polly?" she asked.

"Yes, I think there might be, Mrs Turgoose but I'll just check for you."

"Where did you manage to get jelly from anyway?" she asked as Polly returned holding a small glass dish with a large spoonful of jelly in it.

"Would you believe Mrs Garside managed to find it at the back of a cupboard at The Elms. She said she was saving it for a special occasion, and thought that this was special enough for her."

"Very nice," Mavis slurped the soft jelly over her gums.

"How is Ivy getting on with Harold being away?" Polly asked politely.

"Oh, we're doing alright, Polly. I suppose Ivy misses him, but I'm staying with her for the duration so she won't be lonely."

Polly thought the boot was probably on the other foot, and Ivy's mother was the one who wouldn't be lonely. She had probably moved herself in under the pretext of keeping her daughter company while her husband was away fighting.

"Let's hope it will be over soon then, eh?" Polly commented wryly and she started to wash the dishes.

"What're you going to be doing now that your job's finished."

"Well, I thought I would apply for a job back at The Elms, helping out with the wounded officers."

"Ooh, that's a good idea. I wonder if Ivy might like to do something like that."

"I thought she had a job at Hoppers with Laura."

"Yes, but maybe the pay's better, working for officers, I mean."

"I doubt it, Mrs Turgoose. Factories always pay better than nursing or menial work."

"I suppose so, but I might ask her if she fancies it anyway."

"Ask me what?" Ivy walked into the kitchen and picked up a tea towel to start drying the dishes, a thought that had never crossed her mother's mind.

"Polly's thinking of starting work at The Elms, working with the wounded soldiers. Do you think you might like that?" Mavis asked, a little taken aback to have been caught out talking about her daughter.

"No, I don't! Thank you very much. The sight of blood turns my stomach, so don't go putting my name forward for anything like that, mother."

"Oh, alright, I just wondered that's all."

Polly smiled at the exchange between mother and daughter and guessed that Ivy had her work cut out keeping her mother in her place. It was probably quite a lively household next door. She was looking forward to lodging with Laura while George was away and thought the house on Chapel Lane would be a great place for them to start their married life. If only the war would be over by Christmas like they had said last year.

Chapter 13

The Monday after the wedding saw everything return to normal and Polly moved some of her personal things into the room that Laura had made ready for her. It was larger than the one she was used to on Beck Hill but she still had her old bed and familiar things around her. Also, there was an indoor bathroom and toilet which was absolute heaven, after years of going down the yard or using a chamber pot in the night. George had gone back to the barracks on Sunday night leaving Laura to get on with things as best as she could. There was no time for moping about as she was to start work again herself the next day.

The Labour Exchange had posters asking for nurses and auxiliary nurses to enquire within so Polly joined the queue in the small office and waited for her turn to be called. Her wait was rewarded by her being called to a counter where an officious man with a handlebar moustache waited with his pen poised over a piece of printed paper.

"Land Army is it?" he snapped without looking up.

"No, it isn't," Polly answered firmly.

The man looked up in surprise at the curt retort and blustered, "Don't take that tone with me, young woman."

"Well, don't speak to me in that way yourself, either." Polly was surprised at herself for answering back but didn't flinch from his gaze. Her years in the Beauchamp household had given her a wider vocabulary and a greater degree of confidence.

Eventually, the man looked down at the paper on his desk, put his pen down and looked up at her again with a fixed smile on his face.

"Shall we start again?" he asked.

"I think we'd better, don't you?" she answered firmly smiling back politely.

"How can I help you, Miss... er?"

"Miss Hardcastle, Polly Hardcastle. I would like to know more about joining the auxiliary nursing staff at The Elms. I have worked there for five years as a nanny to little Michael Beauchamp so I know the house and the family. I think I may be of use in some capacity and would like more information, please." She passed her identity papers over the desk to him and waited for a response. After a cursory glance he passed them back again.

"At the moment the house is being fitted out with beds and hospital paraphernalia, so there isn't any nursing work to be done yet. Do you want to train as a nurse?"

"I'm not sure yet, I thought I would do some auxiliary work first and then make up my mind."

"You still have to have training, even to be an auxiliary. You would have to travel to Scunthorpe Hospital every day or Grimsby to receive training and there would be exams to pass. We could find you a billet in either town if you wanted to stay near to the hospital. It might be a while before you could take up any kind of nursing work at The Elms. It is to have a special burns unit too, but I suppose you knew that, knowing the family so well."

"Actually, no, I didn't know that," Polly answered honestly. "I haven't seen Christopher Beauchamp since he went back to Scampton, so I'm a little out of touch. I didn't really want to go away for training as my sister is relying on me staying with her while her husband's away in the army." Polly was in a quandary. She had thought all she had to do was say she wanted to work at The Elms and that would be that. It wasn't going to be as easy as she had anticipated and felt a little foolish. She looked down at her hands resting on the counter and hoped she wouldn't go red and show herself up in front of this man.

"Mr.... I'm sorry - I don't know your name."

"Fletcher," he answered not unkindly. It seemed he wasn't made of stone after all and he patted her hand.

"I tell you what, Miss Hardcastle. What would you say to a job at The Elms but not in a nursing capacity?"

Polly looked heartbroken and answered hesitantly, "What, cleaning you mean?"

"No, not cleaning. You seem an intelligent girl and you're not afraid to speak your mind as I've just witnessed. They will be needing someone in a clerical capacity; someone who will see to the ordering of supplies, making sure the day to day running of the kitchens is in order and that sort of thing. It's a responsible position and one that would suit someone of your experience and knowledge of the running of the house; a bit like a housekeeper if you like."

Polly's eyes shone with relief. "I would love to have a job like that but I didn't know they existed."

"Well someone has to do these things and the matron can't be everywhere at once. You will have to have an interview for the post, of course. Do you think you could manage a job like that?"

"Oh, Mr Fletcher, it would be a dream come true. Thank you for suggesting it and please put me down for an interview. I can attend any time."

For the first time in many long weeks Arthur Fletcher smiled a genuine smile, and handed Polly an application form.

"Shall we fill it in together, Polly?"

"Yes please, Mr Fletcher," she answered thankfully and he was rewarded with the happiest face he had seen for months as they started filling out the form.

When Laura returned home from work that evening she found Polly in the kitchen preparing their meagre evening meal. After calling at the house on Beck Hill after leaving the Labour Exchange, and picking up a very welcome letter from Christopher, and queuing at the butchers for half an hour she had managed to get two lamb chops. Further queuing at the greengrocers produced some new potatoes and spring cabbage which were bubbling away nicely on the gas stove.

"Well, I must say I like having a hot meal to come home to, Polly," Laura said as she walked in through the back kitchen door. "I think this little arrangement will work out nicely for us, don't you?"

"Make the most of it while you can Laura. I've got an interview to go to about a job at The Elms. I've got to wait for a letter telling me when to go."

"Oh, right. Are you going to be nursing so soon?"

"No. I'm not going to be nursing at all. It's a housekeeper come clerical job a man at the Labour Exchange told me about."

Over their meal Polly told her all about Mr Fletcher's suggestions and Laura could see that she was excited about the prospect of the new job.

"Well, I hope it comes off for you, Polly. I bet there will be a lot for it though, so don't get your hopes up too high will you?" Polly's face dropped and Laura was quick to add "I'm not saying you don't stand a good chance though, I think with your experience of the house you should get it easily."

Polly brightened, "Yes, that's what Mr Fletcher said."

Back in her room that evening she opened the letter that had been burning a hole in her coat pocket since the afternoon. It told her everything she had wanted to hear.

My Darling Polly,

I miss you already and I've only been back at camp a day. Although we've known each other for five years on and off, the time we spent in the boat together was truly wonderful. I know Dunkirk was no picnic and we didn't seem to see much of each other as we were so busy dodging bullets and bombs, but the time we did spend together just confirmed my feelings for you.

I know there's a war on and facing facts, I am doing one of the most dangerous jobs I could be doing, I suppose, but would you think very badly of me if I asked you to wait for me, Polly. Will you do that? This war can't possibly last forever and when it's over I want to know that I can come back to you. It would mean so much to me if you would write back and tell me how you feel too.

Please write soon, Polly.
  With love always
   Chris x x x

Polly closed her eyes and hugged the letter to her, reading it again and again just to make sure she hadn't misunderstood anything. She lay back on her bed and thought about what it would mean if she waited for Chris to come back after the war. She would be twenty one years old at the end of the year and Chris would be twenty two. How long could the war last? Up until now the only problems they had had was the queuing for food and shortages of milk and eggs. People were calling it the Phoney War because so far there had been very little damage and children were returning from the country back to the cities as their parents thought they would be safe. She reached for her writing pad and pen and composed her letter.

Dearest Chris

Thank you for your letter which I was so pleased to receive. It's a dream come true to know that you feel the same way about me as I do about you. Of course I will wait for you, but you must promise to be careful in whatever you are doing. Who knows how long we will have to wait until this war ends and we can be together.

I only know that the time we spent together recently was wonderful, even though it was dangerous, I knew I would be safe if you were there. That must mean something, mustn't it?

I have a feeling the war hasn't really started yet but I am going to help as much as I can. I am going back to the Elms for an interview for a job there but not as a nurse – as a housekeeper! I bet you are surprised. I only hope I get the job as I will feel closer to you if I can work there. I am hoping that we will be able to meet up as often as possible but I understand that none of us are our own masters at the moment and you especially, must go wherever you are sent.

I will miss you dreadfully but I hope you can get a weekend pass occasionally and come home to me.

I will be waiting.

With lots of love

Polly x x x

Polly put the letter in an envelope and addressed it to Chris at the address he had put at the top of his letter. She couldn't wait to tell Laura, but decided it would be too late there and then and it would have to wait until the morning. She closed her eyes and fell soundly asleep, dreaming of her dashing young airman and the future that beckoned them.

*****

A couple of weeks later the day of Polly's interview arrived and she dressed as carefully and smartly as possible for the occasion. She had cut her hair to shoulder length and indulged in a Marcel wave. The effect was stunning and gave height at the front. The sides were taken back with two combs and the back turned under and bounced as she walked. With thoughts of Christopher not far from her mind, she clipped on the butterfly earrings he had given her last Christmas. Her smart floral patterned suit had cost her a fortune in coupons and money but she was delighted with the result, her confidence was high as she walked into the hallway at The Elms. She was surprised when Mr Henderson opened the door to her but he explained that Lord and Lady Beauchamp had stipulated that he and Mrs Garside must be kept on if the house was to be used as a hospital. Polly was pleased to hear that at least she knew two faces already.

The scene in front of her was chaos incarnate as the carpets had been stripped out of the hall and metal bed frames were leaning up against the walls. Mattresses were piled high and builders could be heard knocking down walls and judging by the shouts of "turn the tap on again Albert," doing something with the plumbing.

A smartly dressed woman appeared and guided her through the chaos into an inner sanctuary which had been made over into an office. A desk stood in front of one of the long windows and Polly tried to remember what it had looked like before and then realised that a wall had been built dividing one room into two and she was now in the garden room as Lady Beauchamp had called it. It had been a very large room with French windows out into the garden but now was devoid of any of the comfort it had once given.

"Good afternoon, Miss Hardcastle. I'm June Tomlinson and I work for the hospital in a recruitment capacity. I'm just here for the time being to recruit the staff needed to help run this unit and make it ready for the servicemen when they arrive."

"Hello," said Polly politely, not quite knowing what she was supposed to say.

"Please sit down.... Polly isn't it?"

"Yes, that's right." It was like déjà vu as Polly thought back to her first interview all those years ago.

"I have your application form here and it would appear that you made quite an impression on Mr Fletcher at the Labour Exchange. He has told us that you worked here for five years in an entirely different capacity, as a nanny I believe."

"Yes, I enjoyed working here very much and I hoped I might continue to do so in some way."

"Well, I must say it would be helpful to have someone who knows how a large house is run. Mr Henderson is very good but his age lets him down I'm afraid and of course he has no experience of clerical matters."

Polly gulped and looked at her hands. "Neither have I Mrs Tomlinson. I just know that I could be of use here and I would work very hard."

"Can you use a typewriter, Polly?"

"No, I've never tried, but I'm willing to learn."

"You would be required to use one, but I'm sure training would be given to the right candidate."

"Are there many candidates for the job, Mrs Tomlinson?"

"Yes, quite a few, but I must say between you and I, most of them aren't suitable as they think a housekeeper's job is like being a housewife. I don't think they appreciate the amount of responsibility and organisation that will be needed to carry out the duties satisfactorily." June Tomlinson looked at Polly's reaction to this but saw only determination in her eyes.

"Can you explain the duties to me please?"

"I tell you what. Let's take a tour of the house and you can see what is going on, and how things have changed. I'll explain what needs to be done as we go around."

For the next hour Polly was shown around the partially converted house and was pleased to see that the fireplaces and wood panelling on the walls had been boarded over to protect them. She explained to Mrs Tomlinson how she would organise deliveries and order supplies as well as keep on top of the domestic staff to make sure that the wards were spick and span.

June Tomlinson listened to this young girl and realised that she had a quick mind and grasped things well. She had drive and energy and despite her youth and inexperience, she would be perfect for the job. She resolved to recommend her to the matron and would suggest her training started immediately.

When they reached the kitchen Mrs Garside was over the moon that Polly had applied for the job and when it was explained that Polly would effectively be in charge of her, she was all smiles and said that if she had to report to Polly, she had no problem about that whatsoever.

When the interview ended she was asked to wait in the kitchen as the hallway was in such chaos and Mrs Tomlinson went to find matron. She found her on the top floor of the house where Polly's and Amy's rooms used to be. These and others like them had been earmarked for nurse's quarters. Having explained that she thought she had found the perfect woman for the job, matron followed her downstairs to meet her.

Matron was slightly out of breath when they reached the kitchen as she was a little overweight and had had to climb down five flights of stairs, but smiled her thanks when Mrs Garside put a cup of tea in front of her.

She looked hard at Polly who tried not to show her nervousness.

"You seem very young to be a housekeeper," she said, surprised at how young this girl looked.

"I'm almost twenty one, matron, and I'm familiar with the house and some of the staff already. I've worked here for five years and only gave up my post of nanny when Lady Beauchamp went to Canada and took little Michael with her. I know I could fulfil the duties of a housekeeper as they have been explained to me, but I'm happy to help in any capacity."

Her reply was obviously the right one as matron beamed at her saying, "Well, it looks like you have the job then, subject to references of course. You won't mind if we contact Sir Giles or Lady Beauchamp would you – for a character reference of course?"

"No, not at all, matron; I was offered the opportunity of going to Canada with them but my sister is here and I didn't want to leave her."

"Tell them about Dunkirk," Mrs Garside could keep quiet no longer and couldn't help herself from butting in.

"I'm sure they're not interested in that, Mrs Garside." Polly was embarrassed.

"What about Dunkirk?" Mrs Tomlinson put in.

Mrs Garside couldn't stop now she had started, "Well Polly and young master Christopher took his dad's boat all the way to Dunkirk and picked up some of our lads off the beaches, and not only that, they went back again and picked up some more. As luck would have it they even rescued young master Martin and brought him back to Blighty. He's in hospital though with burns to his hands, poor thing."

Polly didn't know whether to laugh or cry but after a cautious glance at the two other women she started to laugh.

"Mrs Garside, I needn't tell them anything now, you've done it for me."

"Well, you're a bit backward in coming forward, Polly, and I think you were very brave." She tucked her hands under her ample bosom and pursed her lips.

Matron laughed and eventually they were all laughing and Polly was receiving congratulations all over again.

Chapter 14

The international arena saw a great deal of action in the following months and a trickle of patients to the hospital soon became a flood. Polly had a baptism of fire. Her days became a minimum of 12 hours as she struggled to keep up with the demands on her time. Nevertheless, as the months went by she became adept at prioritising her workload and made sure that everything ran as smoothly as possible. Occasionally, she found the day had made its way to evening before she had time to draw a breath and she had a day bed brought up from the cellar and put in her office so that she might sleep there. Spare clothes hung behind the door and a toothbrush resided in one of her drawers in readiness for yet another hectic day. Eventually though, a routine was established and she found the time to go and walk in the grounds and speak to some of the servicemen. She found this a welcome change from the hurly burly of the previous months but her heart was tested severely by the sight of badly burned pilots, her thoughts naturally turning to Christopher and the risks he ran.

Christopher had re-trained from bombers to Spitfires and made the adjustment with ease, his innate talent for flying being recognised more and more by his senior officers. Polly on the other hand was even more on edge, fearing that one day he would be a resident at the hospital, or worse. Spitfires though, were in short supply for a time but day by day and hour by hour the factory workforce of England worked steadily to produce these superior aircraft to defeat the German Luftwaffe.

An intensive phase of German bombing began in early August 1940 which involved up to 1,500 aircraft a day targeting airfields and radar stations. By late August the enemy had lost more than 600 aircraft and the RAF only 260 but the toll on experienced pilots was heartbreaking. Towards mid-September though, those brave men in their superior Spitfires had effectively won the Battle of Britain as it became known, by shooting down more German bombers than were being built. The raids on airfields and radar stations ceased but the London Blitz continued and was to last until mid-May 1941. The toll on human life and misery was incalculable.

For the residents of Barton though life went on and almost every Saturday night there was dancing at the Odd Fellows Hall or the Assembly Rooms. The winter of 1940/1941 was harsh but Polly decided that she had had enough of work and no play so made plans with Meg to go to the Odd Fellows Hall one night. George had been home on embarkation leave before being shipped overseas and Laura had found herself pregnant two months later which she said had put paid to her dancing days for a while, so Polly met up with Meg for a rare evening of fun.

They arranged to meet inside the hall as it was far too cold to stand outside. One night just before Christmas 1940 Polly walked into the smoke-filled room and stood at the back waiting for her friend. Five minutes later she was joined by Meg who had had a long walk down from the farm with Richard who had promised to pick her up later and walk back with her. He in the meantime, was going for a drink first.

The band was playing a waltz and the two girls partnered each other as was the norm, with most of the local men being away in the forces, but it wasn't long before they had offers from some of the men to dance with them. It was stuffy in the room and the hazy blue smoke was making Polly's eyes sting. After suffering this for an hour or so and to avoid her feet being trodden on any longer by servicemen with two left feet, she decided to make her way to the door for a breath of air. Meg was enjoying a foxtrot with Brush Cox, a local man whose name had been coined from childhood when his stiff hair had stuck up like a yard brush, so Polly didn't disturb her. She went down the stairs and stood outside just to clear her lungs for a while but it was so cold she turned around after five minutes and was about to go up the stairs when someone grabbed her arm and pulled her into the alleyway at the side leading to the garden at the back of the police station next door. Her heart began to hammer as she thought she was going to be attacked.

"Hello, darling. It's wonderful to see you again after all this time."

Polly was in complete shock as she stared up into Chris's warm, loving eyes and didn't know whether to laugh or cry. She squealed her pleasure and jumped into his open arms, returning his kisses gladly.

"How? When?" her disjointed words tumbled out and she couldn't stop laughing. To have him back even for one night was a luxury she hadn't expected and the night suddenly turned golden for her. "How did you know where to find me? Did Laura tell you I was here? How are you? Why didn't you let me know you were coming?"

"Well, yes I did go to see Laura and she told me you were here with Meg. Secondly, yes I'm fine, and thirdly I didn't know I had a pass until an hour ago. I've hitched a lift with a supplies lorry going to Hull so what could have been better?"

Laura looked up dreamily into his eyes and accepted a long kiss from him, holding tightly to the man she loved and feared she would lose every waking hour of every day. She didn't even know she was shivering but Chris could feel it through her thin pink dress and hurried her inside and up the stairs again.

He took a long look at her in the light of the hall and murmured close to her ear "You look lovely tonight, Polly." She smiled and rewarded him with another kiss before he drew her onto the floor to dance and they swayed in complete unison. For the rest of the night she danced with no-one else. Meg caught her eye at one stage as Polly rested her head on Chris's shoulder and winked her understanding. Meg had managed to ditch Brush and had accepted an invitation to dance from an American pilot, who had joined up at the beginning of the war, just for the excitement of flying. He certainly didn't have two left feet and Meg was in seventh heaven.

As the night drew on and the dancing slowed, the lights dimmed and Chris took Polly onto the floor once more. She thought she had never been so happy. Looking up she saw Betty and Ralph dancing closely and looking into each other's eyes now and again and knew exactly how they were feeling.

She looked up at Chris who leaned down and kissed her gently on the lips. He smiled and again leaned over to murmur into her ear.

"Will you marry me, Polly?"

She pulled away from him slightly and he was afraid he had upset her and pulled her back quickly into his arms. "I'm sorry, Polly. Is it too soon? I know we haven't seen much of each other over the last few months but I'm as certain as I ever could be that I want you to be my wife."

"Oh, Chris, of course I want to marry you. I just don't want to upset your parents by going against their wishes. They'll think I'm not good enough for you."

"No they won't, Polly. Not now. Too much has happened in such a short space of time. Class barriers are coming down now and anyway, if you remember, I never cared much for that sort of tosh. So what's the answer Polly?"

Taking a deep breath before answering she said, "The answer is yes, Chris. I want to be your wife more than anything in the world."

His eyes lit up with pleasure and he picked her up and swung her round and round until she had to beg him to stop. They were laughing so much neither of them noticed the dancing had stopped and people were making their way out of the hall. Meg approached them with the American holding her arm and she announced that Billy was taking her home.

"Richard has been in and found a girl to take home, so I will say cheerio now, Polly. I'm glad Chris has turned up at last. It's been ages since I've seen you laugh so much."

"That's because Chris has asked me to marry him, Meg. I can't believe it. I've said yes of course but it's all happened so quickly."

"Make the most of it then, Polly. Enjoy your happiness and the best of British to you both. I'm so pleased for you."

"Thanks, Meg. I'll make her happy, I promise you," Chris said seriously and Meg was sure her friend would be the happiest bride ever.

Polly and Chris walked home slowly without noticing how cold it was. The paths were slippery with the snow that had been falling for about half an hour, and by the time they reached Chapel Lane where Laura was waiting up for them, they both had a thick covering of wet snow on their coats. The blackout curtains were moved aside and the hall light switched off before she opened the door and they fell inside giggling like a couple of school children. With the door securely fastened and the blackout curtain back in place, she went through to the kitchen where she had boiled the kettle ready to make them a hot drink. Polly and Chris followed her where Polly couldn't keep the news to herself any longer.

"Guess what, Laura? Chris has asked me to marry him and I've accepted. What do you think to that?"

After a second of disbelief Laura was all smiles, "Well, that's a turn up isn't it? Congratulations both of you. I hope you'll be very happy. I'll make some tea to toast the occasion."

Instead, Chris reached inside his greatcoat pocket and pulled out a bottle of champagne with a great flourish. He had visited The Elms when the supply truck had dropped him off in the market place to put his kit bag in his room. Using the key to the wine cellar that his father had entrusted to him, he picked out a bottle of champagne just in case they had cause to celebrate. Polly's eyes were round with surprise and Laura hurried off to find some glasses so that they could celebrate in style. Neither of the girls had even seen a bottle of champagne before let alone tasted it, so when the corked popped with a loud bang they both ducked at the same time and looked at each other and laughed. Chris poured the foaming liquid into three tumblers and they lifted their glasses on high to toast their engagement. Both of the girls laughed when the bubbles went up their noses and Christopher leaned close to Polly saying, "We'll choose a ring together when I next get leave, Polly," and even though neither of them knew when that might be, their happiness was tangible, so Polly wouldn't allow herself to think of anything else that night except how much she loved this handsome young man and how wonderful their future was going to be once this dreadful war was over.

He left the house just after midnight and walked back to The Elms. The snow was quite deep and the wind biting but he was oblivious to it as he let himself into the house that had been his family home all his life. It was strange to see rooms turned over to sitting rooms and hospital wards that had once had completely different functions, but as he climbed the stairs and turned into the private wing of the house, he was still thinking of Polly and how perfectly lovely she was.

After one last visit to his fiancée the following day Christopher and Polly walked to the Market Place together to wait for his lift back to camp. Earlier snowfall had melted and re-frozen leaving the ground treacherous. The time they had spent together had flown and neither of them wanted to say goodbye so soon, but both knew they had no choice. The same scene was being played out in every town and village in the country as sweethearts said their farewells until the next time.

With the usual promises to write as much as possible made, Chris jumped into the lorry and Polly watched it go out of sight and sighed deeply as she turned to make her way back home to Laura. As she scrunched her way along the almost deserted streets, she consoled herself with the fact that at least he was still in England, whereas George was somewhere abroad but Laura didn't know where. She wrote to him often and she had told him about the baby, but as yet she had received no letter back. It must be a million times worse for Laura she thought.

*****

Two more surprises awaited Polly the following day, when she returned to work and neither of them were welcome ones. Her euphoria of the previous weekend was shattered when she learned that the first son of the house, Martin, had returned. His hands had been bandaged heavily for months and now they had been taken off he had taken to wearing white linen gloves. Thanks to Polly's first aid and the layer of petroleum jelly she had used when they first discovered him on board, Martin's fingers were intact, if a little claw-like. The redness of the burns had faded a little and his fingernails had started to grow back. The backs of his hands were apparently scarred but these too would fade in time, but for now they were still angry and sore.

He appeared in Polly's office without knocking wearing his white linen gloves and civilian clothes. Polly was taken aback to see him and almost immediately felt the hostility emanating from him as he stood in front of her desk.

"So, you've wormed your way back into this household again, Polly," he sneered.

She felt that the best way to answer him was to ignore the hostility and treat him as she always had, "Martin, how good to see you again," she lied politely, "How are you? How are the hands? Have they recovered?"

Polly thanked her lucky stars that her months of training and experience in a position of authority within the household had prepared her to deal with difficult people and she was able to look him in the eye and put him off his guard. She wasn't the young servant girl she had once been but if he knew that she was to marry into the family at some point in the future, he would have made it his business to stop it immediately.

"I suppose I should thank you for rescuing me from the sea, but I'm not going to. You should have left me to die rather than leave me with useless hands like this." He waved his gloved hands in front of her face. "I've been invalided out of the army thanks to you and your bravado; I can't fire a gun anymore so I'm no good to anybody."

"Still feeling sorry for yourself then, Martin? You're lucky to be alive and if you can't thank me, the least you can do is thank your brother for risking *his* life for you and the others."

Polly was furious and would have continued to give him the sharp edge of her tongue which he more than deserved, when he turned on his heels and left leaving her open-mouthed and disgusted.

The second nasty surprise for her was the return of Jane Brown who had been Michael's first nanny. Polly's job included meeting with Matron on a daily basis to go through an inventory of medical supplies among other things, so when she knocked on her door she received the usual invitation to enter. Not thinking anything was any different to the normal routine Polly walked in and found Matron behind her desk with a nurse standing in front of her but with her back to the door. The nurse didn't turn around and Polly was about to excuse herself and leave when Matron beckoned her forward and said, "I believe you and Jane are old colleagues, Polly." She indicated the nurse in front of her.

It had been almost five years since Jane had left the household under a cloud but when she turned around and looked Polly in the eye, her brittle smile and cold eyes told her that nothing had changed between them. Again, Polly's experience came to the fore and the smile she gave Jane held no malice and she extended here hand as she moved forward to greet her.

"Well, Jane, what a surprise. I didn't know you would be working here again." She kept her voice light and hoped she didn't reveal too much in her words as Matron watched the encounter. Jane ignored the outstretched hand.

"Why would you? I'm told you work as a clerk here so I doubt Matron would confide in you about staff matters."

The reply was typical of Jane and Polly had steeled herself not to show any reaction, but she did notice the quizzical look from Matron. Polly handed over the papers she was carrying to Matron and excused herself for the time being, adding that she would see her later in the day when she wasn't so busy.

Back in her office Polly sat and thought about her life and wondered how she could go from being on top of the world one minute to being dashed against the rocks of despair the next. She would have to write to Chris and let him know that Martin was home and ask him not to tell anyone about their engagement or trouble would no doubt follow quicker than either of them expected. It took a few weeks before her fears became manifest.

Chapter 15

Matron had been discrete in her enquiries regarding Jane and Polly's difficult relationship but Mrs Garside had filled her in with no holds barred, so at least she had an inkling into what had happened five years before. When she asked Polly if having Jane around would be a problem for her, she was told that as long as Jane stuck to nursing and left her to do her work in peace, then there wouldn't be a problem. Whether Polly actually believed her own words was perhaps up for debate, but she hoped they could get on in a professional capacity.

Jane was a little more forthcoming when Matron asked her the same question, accusing Polly of manipulating Lady Beauchamp to further her own ends. Matron drew her own conclusions but kept them to herself especially given the age difference between the two women. At the start of the war Jane had decided to re-train as a nurse and had become adept if not popular in her tasks. She had trained in three different hospitals including it appeared, the same burns unit where Martin had been a patient. They had recognised each other of course, so when the time came for Martin to return home, he suggested they travel together on the train, and Jane was happy to transfer hospitals in order to act as Martin's private nurse for the journey. She would of course, be expected to work with other patients once at the hospital, but their friendship seemed to continue on a private level much to Polly's surprise.

The first evidence of the tactics they would use came after about six weeks. Polly was expecting a delegation of senior officers who were coming to inspect the facilities and also visit the men. She had ordered supplies of food to cater for the visit and had telephoned her list as usual explaining that further documentation would be handed over on receipt. The officers duly arrived at about 10am and Polly was overseeing the dining room preparations for their meal when Mrs Garside made an unusual appearance at the dining room door, beckoning to Polly.

"What's the matter?" Polly asked with a smile on her face.

"We don't have the food you ordered Polly, nothing has arrived yet." Mrs Garside answered worriedly.

"What! It was supposed to be here by yesterday at the latest. Has anything arrived at all?"

"No, nothing. What shall I give them, Polly? I have some cold cuts from yesterday, or I could make a nice stew with them."

"Hold on, Mrs Garside. I'll ring them and check what's happened."

Returning to her office, she dialled the supplier's number and asked to speak to Mr Harris who usually dealt with her orders.

"Hello, Polly. Is everything alright? Sam said you sounded worried."

"Yes, I am Mr Harris. Our supplies for the officer's lunch haven't arrived. Is there a problem?"

"You mean the order that was cancelled a few days ago?" he queried.

She drew in a sharp breath, "I didn't cancel any order, Mr Harris. The officers are here and we don't have the food to prepare lunch for them."

"Sam received a call a few days ago from the hospital cancelling the order as the visit wasn't going ahead. I'm sorry, Polly but they were the instructions we received. If you didn't cancel them, who did?"

"I've a good idea but no proof. Never mind. Mrs Garside is good at making something out of nothing so she will have to work one of her miracles here today. I think in future, Mr Harris, unless I personally call you and cancel orders then you can take it from me that we need everything you can send us."

"Alright, Polly. I hope it all goes off alright. I'll let Sam know what you've said."

She immediately flew down to the kitchen where Mrs Garside was waiting for instructions.

"Stew it is, Mrs Garside. Make us one of your specials and I'll love you forever. It looks like somebody is trying to get me into trouble here."

"I've got a couple of skinned rabbits, Polly. Them, and the cold cuts from yesterday should make something rib sticking for the brass hats. It's what the lads up in the wards have to eat, so if it's good enough for them, then it's good enough for anybody."

"Thanks, Mrs Garside. You're a marvel. Is there anything good for pudding?"

"I'll come up with something, Polly. Don't worry and don't let that awful Jane get the better of you."

Polly smiled a wan smile and tried not to show how worried this had made her. She went back to her office and tried to dismiss it from her mind but it had taken all the joy from the day. Her mood didn't lighten either when after lunch, Matron called her to her office.

Climbing the stairs she happened to pass Jane who was hurrying along one of the corridors carrying fresh linen. The smirk on her face was enough to make Polly want to slap her, but she controlled herself and knocked on Matron's door. On the command to enter she walked in to find one of the Wing Commanders sitting in one of the seats.

"Polly," said Matron, "thank you for coming. This is Wing Commander Douglas. He has something he wants to say to you."

Polly's heart sank even lower and steeled herself for a dressing down about the rabbit stew. She looked from Matron to the Wing Commander and then down at the floor.

"I just wanted to congratulate you, Miss Hardcastle. I believe you managed to salvage a potentially difficult situation here today when your supplies went AWOL."

Polly couldn't believe her ears and stared open-mouthed at the Wing Commander, before collecting her thoughts. "Why, thank you, sir. I suppose these things happen in war time, but the real credit goes to Mrs Garside who seems to be able to work miracles these days."

"Indeed, Miss Hardcastle, and I will be seeing her later. Firstly, though I wanted to say well done to you and keep up the good work."

With that he left the office and Polly turned to leave, but matron stalled her. "Not yet, Polly. I want a word with you."

She went to stand in front of matron who waved a hand towards the chair recently vacated by the Wing Commander, indicating she should sit.

"I wanted to ask you something and please say no if you feel you must, but believe me it would do me a great favour if you could help."

Polly was intrigued and waited for her to continue.

Matron took a deep breath before continuing, "I know a little of your previous encounters with Jane Brown and I know you haven't always seen eye to eye."

Polly still waited for her to continue, wondering what was coming next.

"It's like this. We have no spare accommodation in the house for staff at the moment, and Mrs Gadie, who is Jane's landlady, has asked me to remove her from her billet for reasons that I can't divulge obviously." Polly could see matron struggling to get her words out so she tried to help.

"Laura doesn't have any spare rooms, matron, and if she had I doubt very much she would let Jane sleep there."

"No, I'm not expecting that she lodge with you and your sister, Polly. What I am trying to ask but not succeeding very well is to ask you if you could possibly rent out the little house you used to live in. I believe it's empty now and it would bring in a couple of shillings rent which would be paid out of Jane's wages so there would be no trouble in this regard."

Polly was stunned to silence. She had no idea what to say. Eventually, she looked around the room for inspiration and said "I don't know, matron. I'll have to discuss it with Laura but Jane is the last person I would really want to live there."

"I know you have issues, but she is such a difficult girl to get along with. I believe that she would be better off living in solitude. I would be very grateful to you and Laura, Polly. Please speak to her about it tonight and let me know tomorrow."

"I will, Matron."

She stood up to leave but turned at the door saying, "I don't really have a problem with Jane, matron. She appears to have a problem with me. I wish we could sort it out but she's really taken against me and I suspect it was her that cancelled my food order the other day."

Matron looked horrified. "I didn't know it had been cancelled, Polly. I thought there had been a mix-up somewhere. Oh, dear. I'm sorry to hear things are being made difficult for you and we must try to be more vigilant in the future."

"I didn't mean to let on, matron, and I can't be certain of course. I just thought you knew."

Polly closed the door quietly and wandered back down to her office. The rest of the day was full of routine paperwork and when Mrs Garside popped in with a cup of tea for her, they both had five minutes together. Mrs Garside was full of what Wing Commander Douglas had said about her rabbit stew. "He really loved it, Polly. Fancy that. A man like him liking rabbit stew. Of course, it did have my special gravy and even some dumplings. He said it was good to know his men were receiving good, wholesome home cooking and they would soon be back on their feet if they continued to eat so well."

"You certainly did a good job, Mrs Garside. It looks like something good came out of it after all."

Polly thought the end of the day could not come quick enough. She couldn't wait to get home and soak her feet. She felt as if she was coming down with a cold as her head was aching and she felt chilled to the bone. At last, she put on her brown checked coat and matching beret, tied her homemade scarf around her neck and made for home. She was pleased she had bought some warm ankle boots for the winter and she wore some thick knitted stockings to keep her legs warm in the chill wind. She had a lot to speak to Laura about tonight and hoped there was something hot waiting for her when she got in.

Opening the back door she saw a note from Laura on the draining board.

"Gone next door, Polly, Mavis isn't well. Come round when you're ready," the note announced. She didn't stop to take her coat off but went through the adjoining gate in the back garden and knocked once before walking into her neighbour's house.

"Hello, Polly. Ivy has made a cup of tea for you and we were thinking of getting some fish and chips for tea. If there's any fish of course," said Laura. Polly took off her coat and sank gratefully into a comfortable armchair by the side of the fire, and accepted a cup of tea.

"How's Mavis, then?" she asked.

Mavis was sat huddled in the other armchair at the other side of the fire. She had a plaid blanket wrapped round her legs and a thick cardigan pulled over her chest. She looked very red in the face and it was obvious she had a temperature. Every now and again she would give a deep chesty cough.

"It's me bronicals, Polly. I'm a martyr to me bronicals and me bunions. Every year's the same. Doctor has given me some medicine though, so I should be up and about soon. Laura has been marvellous, looking after me while Ivy's at work."

"I'm sorry to hear you're not well, Mavis. I think I might have a bit of a cold too." Polly replied. She looked at Laura and continued, "I don't think I fancy fish and chips Laura, sorry. I think I'll drink my tea and then go home and soak my feet for a while. You stay if you like."

"No, don't be silly. Ivy's home now so I'll come home with you when you've finished your tea."

Polly looked gratefully at her sister and drank the last of her tea in two gulps. She stood up to go, but swayed when her head started to throb.

"Looks like you'd better get her to bed with a hot water bottle, Laura," Ivy observed. "Do you want some help?"

"That's alright, Ivy. I'll manage. I feel like Florence Nightingale today," Laura smiled as she guided Polly through the back gate and into their own cosy back kitchen. Once there, she sat Polly down in front of the banked up fire after taking her coat and hat off, and eased her feet out of her boots.

"You look really pale, Polly. Should I send for the doctor?"

"No, that's alright. I just need a bit of a rest. I have to ask you something as well."

"Whatever it is can wait till you're soaking your feet. They're freezing in them boots."

One of the advantages of living in Chapel Lane was that it had running water laid on into the house. The little house on Beck Hill had been served by a pump in the back garden which they had had to share with the Taylors next door. Previously, they had had to have a bath in front of the fire using an old zinc bath that hung on a nail on the back of the shed door, so this house was infinitely more luxurious to them.

Laura brought a bowl full of warm water into the sitting room and placed Polly's feet into it. She poked the fire into life and watched as her sister began to relax. She went back into the kitchen and returned a few minutes later with a couple of aspirins and a glass of water, which she made her take. She picked up a crocheted blanket that usually lay on the back of the sofa and wrapped it cosily around Polly's shoulders. Satisfied that she had done everything she could, she sat opposite her and waited for her to speak.

Polly told her what had happened at work that day and Laura's face was livid when she heard about the dirty trick Jane had pulled, but laughed when she realised that it had all worked out well in the end. When Polly broached the subject of Jane living in the house at Beck Hill, Laura was silent for a long time, thinking over the situation.

"I think it might be just the thing for her, Polly. George's mam and dad are moving to Ramsden Avenue soon, so there'll be nobody for her to fall out with. Just think, Polly. She'll have to use the pump in the yard to get water, and have a bath in that awful zinc bath. It's what she deserves after what she's done to you today, and don't forget the newts crawling up the passage."

Polly laughed out loud and then grimaced as pains shot through her head. Laura stood up and took the bowl of water out into the kitchen again to empty it, returning with a towel to wipe her sister's feet. They felt warmer now and Polly had a bit of colour in her cheeks, but Laura wasn't sure if it was a temperature or not.

"Come on, let's get you to bed. I'll bring you a hot drink and a hot water bottle up."

Polly stood up and shuffled up the stairs to her bedroom. The chimney from the downstairs fire went up through her room so it was quite cosy and warm in there. Laura closed the thick curtains over the black-out curtains which let no light through and Polly settled down while Laura went to fetch her a hot water bottle. When she got back Polly was already drowsy so she pushed the stone hot water bottle under her feet and tucked her in for the night, kissing her on the forehead as she had done since they were children.

"Night, night, Polly. Hope you're better in the morning."

Polly murmured her thanks and turned over to go to sleep.

Chapter 16

Polly slept for almost twenty four hours and when she woke up Laura was sat by her bed with a damp cloth in her hand which she immediately used to wipe the beads of sweat of Polly's forehead. When she tried to get up on one elbow she found that every joint in her body ached and Laura had to help her by propping pillows behind her back while offering a drink of cool water.

"Thanks," was all she could croak through her swollen and sore throat.

"Well I'm glad to see you're back in the land of the living. I thought you were going to sleep forever."

Polly lolled back against the pillows, her body protesting at every movement.

"How long have I been asleep?" she whispered, trying not to move her head which felt thick and heavy.

"It's Tuesday night. You've slept the day through and hopefully you'll sleep again soon and try and get better. You've got a really bad dose of the 'flu."

"I think I need to go to the bathroom, Laura. Will you help me?"

"Do you think you can manage it?"

"I'll have to or I'll wet the bed."

With great gentleness Laura helped her into the bathroom and then returned to the bedroom and changed the sheets quickly as they were soaked with perspiration. Polly was shivering when she returned to fetch her from the bathroom and so a change of nightdress was in order, but before putting it on Laura helped Polly to wash herself before getting into bed again. Feeling a bit more refreshed and sliding into clean sheets felt like heaven and she looked a little better than she had done over the past twenty four hours. What Laura hadn't told her was that she had been delirious during the previous night and shouting out for Christopher, her mother and father, and of course Laura herself.

"I'm going to fetch you a drink of tea and some more aspirins. Can you eat anything?"

"No, I'd love the tea though," she croaked.

"If your throat's no better in the morning I'm going to send for the doctor."

Laura went downstairs to fetch the tea and tablets and Polly relaxed again against the pillows. She had had colds before but this was something altogether different and hoped Laura wouldn't catch it as she was five months pregnant now and although not too big yet, she was obviously showing now despite the smocks she wore.

"I'll be alright now, Laura," she said as she came into the room with a tray holding two cups of tea and a glass of water. "You must look after yourself and the baby I don't want you to get this cold."

"I'll just have a cup of tea with you and let you know what I've done today and then I'll leave you to sleep and I'll go to bed as well."

Polly listened while Laura explained that she had been to see Matron at The Elms and told her that Polly was unwell and wouldn't be back to work for at least a week, maybe even more. Normally Polly would have been horrified at this, but just at that moment she felt as if she wanted to stay in bed forever, so she didn't protest. Laura went on to explain that she had taken the keys to the house on Beck Hill and given them to matron to pass on to Jane on the understanding that the rent would be two shillings per week and she would have to furnish the place herself but she could use whatever bits and pieces she and Polly had left behind. Matron had been all smiles and told her that the rent would be paid to you personally when you returned to work and matron herself was going to organise a rent book.

"Just think, Polly. She's going to have to get that kitchen stove lit again after all this time and the fire in the sitting room will need to be lit too. If she needs the chimney swept she'll have to do that herself. That'll teach her to be nasty to you."

Polly was so weak she almost cried with gratitude that Laura had sorted it out for her. All she could do was give a watery smile.

"You settle down now, love. I'll see you in the morning and I hope you're feeling a lot better by then." Laura could see how tired she was so she took her cup from her and watched her take the aspirin, leaving her to sleep. Polly was instantly asleep and didn't even move when Laura pushed the hot water bottle wrapped in a towel under her feet again.

Polly's 'flu lasted just over a week but it took nearly another week for her to recover enough to return to work. When she returned she was thinner and paler than ever, and matron was afraid she had returned too soon. A young man who had been declared unfit for the services had been helping out in the office doing the routine work and keeping things ticking over, but he was glad to see Polly return and take over the reins again. His name was Eric Farr and he had had a heart murmur from birth. He had been declared medically unfit to fight - which he was far from happy about. Instead, he had to be content with joining the Home Guard which had been formed in the May of 1940, initially going by the name of the Local Defence Volunteers.

He gave Polly a rundown of his duties with the Home Guard which included fire watching at the local factories and helping to guard the shoreline against invasion. They also patrolled the town and surrounding areas looking out for enemy parachutists and generally being helpful to the regular army and alerting them if anything unusual happened. Polly listened with half an ear as she was quite familiar with the role he played but she pricked up her ears when she heard him mention that Martin had joined too. Further first hand evidence of this met her eyes when later that afternoon she saw him leaving the house in uniform accompanied by Eric.

Matron tapped at her door as she was preparing to leave for the evening.

"Polly, sorry I haven't been able to see you today. It's been one of those days I'm afraid. We've just had six more patients admitted today, poor souls, it seems like we're on a treadmill at the moment. What I came to ask you was whether or not you would like to keep Eric as an assistant?"

Polly thought for a moment. "Yes, I think I would please, matron. He's been very useful in doing some of the routine work and leaves me time to deal with more pressing matters. Mrs Garside says he's even helped her out in the kitchen when she's needed it; so I think he would be an asset."

"Jolly good. I'll let him know tomorrow. How have you settled back in? Is everything alright?"

"Yes, just a bit of a backlog in clerical matters but otherwise Eric has done a good job holding the fort for me."

"Good, I'm glad about that. Jane has settled into your old house by the way. I believe Martin Beauchamp has helped her to get some second hand furniture. They seem to be getting on well."

Polly didn't remark one way of the other, so Matron took the hint and went back to her office. Polly wondered how long it would be before she regretted letting Jane rent the old house. She was brought out of her reverie when then the phone rang.

"Polly, is that you?"

"Chris! How lovely to hear from you. You've just caught me before I leave. Is everything alright?"

129

"Yes, fine. I just wanted to tell you that I'm being promoted and I'm transferring back to bombers soon. Guess where I'll be stationed."

"Not Scotland I hope."

"No, Elsham. I'm going to be on the doorstep Polly. We'll be able to meet up a lot more. Isn't that wonderful?"

"That really is the best news I've had for ages, Chris. When will you be coming home?"

"Not too sure. I've got to go on another course. I'm going to be Pilot Officer Beauchamp with my own crew. I should be back by the summer though. Are you better, Polly? I was sorry to hear about the 'flu."

"Yes, I'm fine thanks. I can't wait for your transfer Chris. It can't be soon enough. I miss you so much."

"Me too. Got to go now, Polly. Love you."

With that the phone went dead at the other end and she put the phone down. Just then she heard a noise outside the door and went to investigate. Looking out down the corridor she saw a nurse walking away but couldn't be sure who it was.

*****

Laura's baby girl was born one hot day in June 1941. She was to be called Emma after George's mother and she seemed happy with the name. Her good nature was apparent from the day she was born, causing the midwife, Nurse Beswick, to remark that she had never seen a first baby born so easily. Laura would have argued about that, but she was overjoyed to hold her new baby in her arms after just six hours of labour. To her they were the longest six hours she had ever had to endure but the reward was worth every agonising minute.

Polly was her first visitor. She looked into the tiny face with wonder. She counted her little fingers and toes and wrapped her in a shawl promising to walk the floor with her if she cried at night, allowing Laura have some well-deserved sleep between feeds.

Neighbours visited frequently and two of George's sisters, Marie and Evelyn, were frequent visitors. They had got their wish and stayed occasional weekends in the spare room and loved to help Laura with baby Emma.

About six weeks after Emma's birth Laura and Polly were taking a well earned rest in the garden, making the most of the August sunshine. It was one of those summer days when the breeze was just cool enough to make it bearable to sit in the sun. Next door's cat was sleeping precariously on the shed roof and all was quiet as the girls chatted comfortably until Mavis, now well and truly recovered from her attack of bronchitis, joined them from next door.

"Now then, Laura," she began, heaving her bulk into an old deckchair they had found in one of the outhouses. "I just wanted to know when you were thinking of having Emma christened, 'cos I've got my eye on a nice new hat. It's in Esme Pratt's window on the High Street, and it's quite reasonable considering."

"We were just discussing that, Mavis," Laura replied. "The vicar's coming round tonight."

"Ooohh, good. I like a nice christening. Are you getting churched at the same time?"

"I think so, but I hope it doesn't take too long."

"No, not long at all and then we can enjoy the christening."

Mavis had obviously taken it for granted that she would be invited to the gathering and Laura didn't have the heart to disillusion her. Ivy and Mavis had been good neighbours, especially when Polly had been so ill during the winter months it was the least they could do.

"I'll let you know when and you can keep that Sunday free, Mavis. I just wish George could get leave to be with us, but he's over in Africa at the moment and has been since last year. I pray every night he will come home soon alive and well."

"We all pray that lass. Ivy is missing Harold like mad but I try to keep her from moping about. We have a good laugh now and again, usually at somebody else's expense."

Polly returned from a trip to the kitchen with three cups of tea.

"Where's Ivy, Mavis? Does she want to join us for a cuppa to you think?"

"She's gone into work to do some overtime, but she'll be back later. I'll tell her about the christening when she gets back."

"Why do people have to be churched? It seems like a really old fashioned way of going on to me," Polly asked.

"To tell you the truth, it is very old fashioned. Anybody would think women were lepers the way they carry on," answered Mavis.

"Why don't you ask the vicar tonight, Polly?"

"That's a good idea, I think I will."

Just then Emma started to cry for her dinner and the peace and quiet was shattered for a while. Laura took her indoors to feed her and Mavis went back home. Polly sat for a while day dreaming about

Christopher and wishing he was there with her. She must have fallen asleep because the next thing she knew Laura was calling her in for her tea.

The vicar arrived promptly at seven o'clock and the christening was arranged for three weeks time at the beginning of September. Polly brought up the subject of Laura being churched before the christening and asked the vicar what it meant.

"It's a ceremony that dates back well into the middle-ages, Polly," he explained. "The ritual is based on a biblical reference in Leviticus where a woman who gives birth to a son is counted as ritually unclean for 40 days and for twice as long after the birth of a female child. After that period of purification she is to go to the temple and bring the required offerings for the priest to make atonement for her. We don't now differentiate between boy or girl children but we still use the ceremony to re-introduce new mothers into their spiritual life."

"Well it seems really old fashioned to me, vicar. After all, child birth is a very natural event so why would Laura or anyone else for that matter, need to be purified afterwards?"

"I see your point, Polly, and I agree with you, but as far as the Christian church is concerned, we still have to follow the rules. Try and think of it as another reason to celebrate Emma's birth."

"I suppose so, vicar. Thanks for explaining it to me."

"You're very welcome, my dear." He stood up to go, handing his empty tea cup to Laura as he headed for the kitchen door. "For a small town we seem to be having christenings most weeks now," he chuckled. We've got three on the same Sunday as little Emma's but we'll get the churching ceremony out of the way before everyone else arrives. Can you be there at 2 o'clock and we'll start the christenings at 2.30?"

"Yes, of course. There will be George's family and Mavis and Ivy Turgoose from next door as well as me and Polly."

He nodded his approval as he left the house. He had no sooner got to the front gate when Mavis put her head round the back door.

"Well, when's it going to be then?" she asked with no preamble.

Laura laughed at her enthusiasm. "The first Sunday in September, Mavis, so you'd better get your skates on and get that new hat before somebody else snaps it up."

"I will. I'll go and get it first thing Monday morning. It's the first thing we've had to celebrate since your wedding, Laura. I can't wait." She turned and headed back home to let Ivy know what was going on.

132

The christening took place in St Mary's church on a perfect late summer's day. The sky was azure blue and the sun shone as if giving a blessing on baby Emma. It wasn't too hot, or too cold, and Mavis got the chance to wear her new hat, a pink and white creation which looked a bit like a meringue, but surprisingly suited her perfectly. Everyone from George's family was in attendance except for the sons of the family as they were all away fighting for their country. Ralph was the only exception as he was given a weekend pass, and he brought Betty along as a guest.

The churching ceremony went ahead without a hitch and after a couple of psalms and a few prayers Laura was once again an accepted member of the church and society as a whole. Polly found it all a bit patronising but entered into the spirit of things for Laura's sake. To her boundless joy Christopher had turned up in time for the ceremony and she held his hand tightly as if she wasn't ever going to let him go again. Laura was stoic in her determination to enjoy the day without George but couldn't help but wish he was there to witness his daughter's christening. Unfortunately, Christopher was only able to attend the ceremony and had to head back straight away, but at least he had made the effort to get there and Polly was glad of every minute she could spend with him.

After the service everyone from the group had been invited to go for Sunday lunch to the Taylor's new house in Ramsden Avenue. It was a council property but they had four bedrooms which allowed the privacy that had been lacking on Beck Hill. One of the bedrooms jutted out over the neighbour's house and provided a few laughs for the older girls when they heard their arguments filtering through the ceiling, but it was all good natured fun as far as they were concerned.

Everyone had contributed something to the traditional lunch, and although meat was in short supply, the Dig for Victory campaign meant that vegetables were available for everyone. Mrs Taylor, Emma's namesake, was kept busy in the kitchen but there were plenty of willing hands to help dish out her delicious lunch. She was a small, delicate lady who always kept a nice, clean and tidy house – a feat in itself considering how many people passed through it daily.

After lunch had been cleared away and the washing up done, Polly joined the two youngest girls, Marie and Evelyn, the latter known to her family as 'our Ev', for a walk with Emma in her pram, leaving

Laura and George's mother to have a rest. They had just started to walk up Stivvy Hill when Eric Farr caught her up. He was in his Home Guard uniform and carried a rifle which greatly impressed the younger children.

"Hello, Polly. It's a lovely day isn't it?"

"Hello, Eric. Yes, it's beautiful. What are you doing in uniform? Aren't you hot?"

He pulled a face, "I'm boiling, but I'm on duty so I have to wear it. I just wish it wasn't so scratchy."

She felt sorry for him but thought of George. "At least you're not in Africa. It could be worse."

"Yes, you're right and I should be thankful for small mercies."

"Is this your usual patrol area then or are you training?" she asked as they were some distance from the town and surrounded by countryside.

"No, not really," he explained. "There was a raid on Hull a couple of nights ago and we've been told to look out for a couple of German pilots that might be wandering about. Somebody reported them bailing out after their aircraft was hit. I don't think you should be walking up here today, Polly. Not until we either find them or it's proved that nobody survived the crash."

Polly shuddered and looked around her. Marie and Ev were pushing Emma's pram a few yards in front and she thought they ought to turn round and go back home but she didn't want to alarm them. They were nearing the top of the hill where it joined Horkstow Road which would take them back into Barton so she decided to carry on. At the junction Eric went in the opposite direction with a cheery wave saying, "See you at work tomorrow morning."

Polly hurried the girls on and they reached Brigg Road without mishap, but she was constantly looking in ditches as she walked and was relieved to see Baysgarth Park in the near distance.

She sat under a tree while Ev and Marie went to the swings, although they were both getting too old for playgrounds, and waited for them to return. The afternoon was cooling into evening when they came back breathless after their exertions so, because they were hot and thirsty and Emma needed changing, they made their way home to Ramsden Avenue.

Ivy and Mavis had gone home by the time they arrived back and Laura was glad to see Emma again. She hadn't been parted from her for more than five minutes since she was born, so a whole afternoon without her had left her anxious. Polly was sorry she had been out so long when she saw the concern on Laura's face but after a cooling drink, they made their way home and Polly told her about the enemy pilots, but Laura was dismissive and thought it was all a figment of somebody's overactive imagination. Nothing like that ever happened in Barton. It was such a sleepy little town and if it wasn't for the food shortages, and the men being absent, it hardly seemed like there was a war going on at all. Polly thought of the injured men at the hospital but didn't say anything, putting Laura's mood down to being worried about Emma.

*****

When Polly arrived at work the next day she found Matron waiting for her in her office.

"Good morning, Polly. How did the christening go? I hope it all went well."

"Yes, thank you, Matron. We had a lovely time and Emma was really well behaved."

"Good, good." Matron seemed somewhat edgy prompting Polly to ask if she was alright.

"I've got something to tell you, Polly. It's Eric...."

Polly's intake of breath was audible and she looked nervously at Matron.

"He's missing," she continued. "It would appear that he was patrolling yesterday afternoon as ordered, but he never reported in before he left for the evening. His mother says his bed hasn't been slept in."

"Oh no, I saw him yesterday afternoon. We were taking Emma for a walk up Stivvy Hill and he walked with us to the top. We turned left and he turned right. He said he would see me at work today."

Polly's eyes filled with tears and her voice was unsteady as she spoke.

"I do hope he's alright, matron. He said he was looking for a couple of German pilots that had bailed out a few nights ago after a raid on Hull."

"I'll call his commanding officer and tell him what you've told me, Polly. Maybe it will help."

Matron picked up the phone on Polly's desk and dialled the operator, asking to be put through to the Drill Hall on Butts Lane.

After explaining to someone who she was she was finally put through to the duty commander. She explained what Polly had told her and he said he would come over and interview her himself. Half an hour later she was sat with a cup of tea to calm her nerves, relaying the story to a man she had never seen before. He was tall and well spoken with the darkest eyes she had ever seen on a man. His thick moustache drooped at the corners giving him a foreign look.

He asked Matron to close the door to the office and lowered his voice as he spoke to Polly.

"Now then young lady, I'm Colonel Da Silva and I want you to listen very carefully to what I am going to tell you, and then I want you to forget you ever heard it. Do you understand me? It is of the utmost importance that no-one else is privy to what I am going to tell you."

Polly nodded her head and took a gulp of her tea. She wished for all the world that she hadn't bothered going into work that morning. Poor Eric. Where could he be? Her eyes began to fill up again and Matron passed her a handkerchief. Just then there was a knock on the door and she nearly jumped out of her skin as Martin Beauchamp entered, saluting the officer in the room. After a perfunctory salute the officer indicated that he should stand by the door. This worried Polly even more. What on earth was going on? Why didn't they just get on with it and tell her. What had it to do with Martin?

"Right, we're all here now so here goes," he looked Polly in the eye as he tried to explain. "You are acquainted with Captain Beauchamp here, aren't you?"

Polly nodded and didn't say anything about not knowing Martin was a Captain.

"What you won't know is that Captain Beauchamp is working under cover for British Intelligence." He allowed Polly a moment of stunned silence before continuing. "We have put the Captain here for the purpose of gathering intelligence on any fifth columnist activities in the area and he has been keeping a very close eye on someone else of your acquaintance."

"Who?" she gasped, looking from one to the other for answers.

It was Martin who answered, "Jane Brown."

"Jane!" she exclaimed, the shock showing on her face. "But, she's just a nurse, isn't she?"

"That's what she would like us to believe, Polly. When I was in the hospital in Devon, she was under suspicion then. When my father came to visit me and I was recovering from my burns, he suggested I might like to keep an eye on her, so I befriended her hoping to gain her confidence. She's very good, Polly. She doesn't let anyone get too close to her and as you've noticed, she is deliberately rude to keep people at a distance. We think she knows something about Eric's disappearance and also about the German pilots who bailed out the other night."

"Oh, my goodness, poor Eric. Have you arrested her? What are you going to do? "

Martin took a deep breath and moved closer to her chair. "It's more of a case of what are we going to do, Polly."

"We?" she gasped, "What do you mean?"

"Jane isn't here today and we don't want to go to the house on Beck Hill or we might frighten her off. First of all, I want you to come with me to the last place you saw him yesterday. While we walk up there, I want to explain a few things to you and hopefully you will be a brave girl and agree to help us out."

"If it'll help Eric, I'll try."

She stood up and collected her jacket from the coat peg in the corner and the Colonel stood up with her. Martin saluted smartly and he reciprocated, smiling at Polly saying, "Good girl. We knew we could count on you. The captain here will fill you in on the details. Matron is aware of what is going on so you can talk freely in front of her. When this operation is over though, remember what I told you, *do not* breathe a word of this to anyone – not even your sister."

Polly nodded her agreement and followed Martin out of the door.

As they walked through the park they re-traced Polly's journey of the previous day in reverse. At first conversation was a little stiff but gradually she realised that Martin was speaking to her without any of the malice or spite of their previous encounters so she began to relax.

"I want to apologise, Polly. I've been absolutely horrid to you over the past months but please believe me that it was just an act. I had to appear to be on Jane's side or she might have put two and two together. She's a very intelligent woman, but somehow twisted in her mind. I'm sorry if anything I've said or done has caused you any upset or hurt. Will you forgive me?"

She didn't have to think twice as the apology was so sincere, "Of course I'll forgive you, Martin, and especially so if you can find Eric. I pray that he's safe somewhere and they haven't hurt him." Her voice began to quiver again and Martin put his arm around her to encourage her to be brave. After a moment she said, "I'm alright now, thank you. I'll try not to let it upset me, but he's such a pleasant lad and always very helpful in the office."

They turned right into Horkstow Road and continued along up the hill to the junction where Eric had parted company with them the day before. Instead of going back down Stivvy Hill they continued along the lane hoping to find some trace of the lost Eric.

The countryside was dotted with gorse bushes and a small copse here and there, but mostly the land was turned over to agriculture with fields now shorn of their crops, leaving spiked stubble behind. Flocks of seagulls and rooks dotted the landscape searching for anything that might provide a decent meal and the two young people shaded their eyes against the sun as they scoured the fields for any signs of Eric. How far they walked neither of them knew, but it must have been two hours later when Polly spotted something sticking out of a bush down a bridle path. Running as fast as they could, they came upon a parachute which had obviously been pushed hurriedly into the bushes to try and conceal it. Polly was out of breath but now she was excited to be taking part in this operation and her eyes sparkled with pleasure at their find.

"There, I knew we'd find something. You're a good luck mascot, Polly."

She wasn't too sure about that but immediately beamed with pleasure. "What do we do now, do we take it with us or what?" she asked.

"Good question," he replied stroking his chin as he thought, "I think we'll push it back into the bush and post patrols in the area at night to keep an eye out in case someone comes back to pick it up."

They pushed the parachute back into the bushes and concealed it from view as best they could. "I think we need to keep looking for any further clues," he said as they continue down the bridle path.

As they walked along, the path narrowed to a track for about a hundred yards and then opened up into a perfectly circular earth work with deep, sloping sides. At the bottom was a copse of trees which had provided children with endless hours of fun over the years playing hide and seek. Evidence of their fun and games came in the shape of deep ruts of grassless mud which had baked in the September sunshine. Most of the children were back at school now so the area was deserted but Martin was insistent that they go down for a look around. He went first and helped Polly to follow, her summer sandals proving to give a good grip on the crumbling earth. Something caught the corner of her eye as she looked at the ground, "Look, Martin. Something's shining over there on the ground."

She pointed to her right and he let go of her hand to investigate. He picked up a shiny metal object which on closer inspection turned out to be a button from a Home Guard uniform. Polly looked at Martin and he stared back, neither of them wanting to voice their fears.

"Come on, let's keep going," he whispered holding her gaze as if needing her permission.

"Right, let's go," she answered decisively but in hushed tones.

At the bottom of the dip there were more gorse bushes and a few stunted trees. Polly was out of breath and looked back up the slope, wondering how on earth she was going to climb out again. As a child she had run up and down these slopes countless times, but now the effort looked beyond her.

They followed the circular edge of the copse and then she remembered an old track which they used to follow as children which led to the centre of the trees. Pulling Martin behind her they bent almost double forcing their way through the overgrown bushes, branches and thorns pulling at their clothes as they went. At last, they reached the centre where the trees gave way to a grassy clearing. There at the edge of the grass and almost concealed by an overhanging bush was the body of a man wearing nothing but underwear and socks. His face was turned away from them and Martin urged Polly to stay where she was as he crept forward. He drew an automatic pistol from his holster and moved forward slowly and steadily. As he drew nearer he could see that the man was bound at the feet with rope and his hands were tied behind his back. He appeared to have a gag in his mouth and Martin prayed to God that if this was Eric, that he was still alive.

He reached the man and kneeled down to look at his face. It was indeed Eric and he beckoned Polly to join him. She approached cautiously but Martin had already put his pistol away so she assumed everything must be alright. Martin felt Eric's neck for a pulse and was pleased to find a shallow throbbing.

"Quick, Polly. Help me untie him. We need to get some medical attention for him as soon as possible."

By the time they had undone the ropes and gag, and pulled him deep into the shade of the copse, she was shaking with the adrenaline pumping through her system.

"Polly," Martin broke the silence between them. "Will you be alright to stay here with him on your own while I go for help, or do you want to go?"

"No, that's alright. I'll stay here and talk to him if he wakes up. You'll be quicker than me. Go back down Horkstow Road and head up to the Parker's farm it's closer than The Elms. They've got a phone."

"Right, I'm off then. Stay here and don't try anything heroic. Just stay put. Understand?" His face was stern as he spoke.

She nodded her understanding and made herself comfortable leaning on a tree next to Eric. Satisfied that she wouldn't do anything to worsen the situation, Martin left her forcing his way back through the tunnel of bushes at a gallop, taking the sides of the slope with large strides. He stopped at the top to get his breath for a few seconds and then ran as fast as he could in the direction of Parker's farm.

Chapter 18

Polly manoeuvred Eric's head onto her lap and talked to him, stroking his hair away from his eyes. Occasionally, he flinched as if she had hurt him and his eyes flickered open but closed again immediately. She was reassured that at least he was still alive and unconsciously began to pray.

She lost all concept of time as the sun travelled overhead but guessed it must be lunch time as her stomach had started to growl quite noisily. She estimated that Martin had been gone about half an hour when she heard someone approaching through the thicket of branches and hoped it was him coming back with help. She edged forward as near to the edge of the trees and bushes as she could but instead, was horrified to see that Jane stood in the middle of the clearing with a man wearing what looked like Eric's Home Guard uniform. Trying not to move too much, she peered out through the bushes which she hoped hid her and the unconscious Eric from obvious view. Jane and her companion were about twenty yards away and she could hear the murmur of their voices but not clearly enough to know what they were saying.

Jane was looking around her and when she looked in Polly's direction she thought she had been spotted and drew back startled. Her quick movement caused a bird to fly out of the bushes and across the clearing into the trees on the other side. Jane watched it as it flew and said something to the other man who laughed in response. Polly was transfixed. She didn't know what to do but remembering her promise to Martin to stay put, she did just that and very, very slowly returned to Eric's prone form, this time praying he would stay asleep so as not to make any noise.

Unfortunately, he chose that moment to make his return to the land of the living heard, and screwed up his eyes as he groaned. He opened his eyes to find Polly shushing him into silence but he was still too far gone to understand what she was trying to say to him. He recognised her immediately, but couldn't understand what had happened to his clothes.

"Hello, Polly. My head doesn't half hurt. What are you doing here? Where's my clothes?" he questioned, far too loudly for Polly's comfort.

"Be quiet, Eric. For goodness sake *be quiet*." She put her finger over his lips and turned around apprehensively when she heard movement in front of her but it was too late, Jane stood with her hands on her hips looking maliciously pleased to find them at her mercy.

She spoke rapidly to her cohort in what Polly assumed was German and he moved purposefully forward, pulling her arms behind her back painfully. She shouted out in agony and Eric started to get up, ready to put up a fight, but when Jane produced a handgun, he thought better of it and sat down again with his hands in the air. The German pilot pushed Polly down next to Eric and smiled wickedly when she winced as the bark of the tree scraped her back.

"Well, well, well – Miss Polly Hardcastle. I have you at my mercy at last," she sneered. "I might have known you would be playing the heroine and rescuing the helpless soldier."

Polly said nothing but hoped that Martin would arrive soon with help.

Jane indicated the man in Eric's uniform, "This is Hans. He's my friend and has come to help me with my work here."

"What work?" Eric asked, more confused than he realised.

"You're nothing but a traitor, Jane Brown," Polly found her voice at last.

"Not so, miss goody two shoes. I am German, born and bred. My name is Erika von Braun and I am proud to be helping the Fatherland in this war. We will have you beaten in no time at all."

Eric was incensed. "That's what you think. We'll fight you everywhere - on the beaches, on the land, in the air or on the sea, just like Mr Churchill said we would. We'll never surrender to you murdering Germans."

Jane's eyes grew large and her face contorted with hatred as she pointed her gun at Eric and fired. Polly screamed, "No," but it was lost in the sound of the shot. She had thrown herself forward instinctively to protect Eric and felt pain in her shoulder and then blackness closed around her.

She regained consciousness when she felt a cold damp cloth on her forehead and choked momentarily as water was trickled into her mouth and down her throat. She couldn't think where she was for a minute but then she heard familiar voices and opened her eyes to see Martin gazing at her with concern. She tried to move but found the pain too much. Eric was fully clothed in civvies but they were still in the copse, that much she could feel as the branches and twigs scratched her legs.

She jumped when she heard a rifle shot and grabbed Martin's sleeve. "What's happened, Martin?" she asked, her eyes clouding with pain.

"You've been shot, Polly. Keep still. We're going to stretcher you out of here."

"But, I just heard another shot. Is Eric alright?"

Eric knelt down beside her, "I'm fine, Polly, thanks to you. I don't know what I would have done if you had been killed when the bullet was meant for me. What would Laura have said?"

Polly smiled as she allowed the stretcher bearers to lift her onto an army stretcher but passed out again as they struggled up the slope with her.

When she next came round she was in a clean hospital bed at The Elms with Matron fussing around her and Laura sitting pale-faced on a hard-backed chair next to the bed. Her relief to see Polly open her eyes was total and she began to cry into her handkerchief.

"Oh, Polly, thank goodness you're alright. I thought you were going to die, even though they told me it was a flesh wound, you looked so poorly."

Matron came over to the bed, "That's because she had lost a lot of blood. Now you can rest up and regain your strength. Eric is going to cover your job until you are better. He wants to see you, Polly. Are you up to it?"

"I want to talk to Laura first, Matron. Is that alright?"

"Of course you can. There's no rush – just take your time. You have been very brave, Polly, and we are all extremely proud of you."

Laura started to cry again and Polly put out her good hand to pat her arm and reassure her.

"I'm going to be alright, Laura. Don't cry. I'll be up and about in no time you'll see." She looked at Matron. "Can we have a cup of tea please?"

"There what did I tell you, Laura? I told you she would be giving me orders soon enough." She laughed as she left the room to give orders for tea and what passed for biscuits to be brought up to Polly.

"Aren't you the pampered one, then? Laura said smiling, feeling reassured. "You've got a private room here all to yourself, courtesy of your fiancée of course. He instructed that his room was made over for your personal use. He is coming over as soon as he can get compassionate leave.

"Martin doesn't know about Chris and me," Polly said, quite alarmed that he would find out this way.

"Oh, yes he does," Martin said as he entered the room carrying a tray with three cups of tea and some biscuits that Mrs Garside had baked herself, "and I couldn't be happier about it, Polly. Congratulations."

"How did you find out?" I never breathed a word to anyone except Laura and Meg.

"You forget I'm in the intelligence business, Polly. I make it my business to know everything," he tapped his nose meaningfully.

"Don't lie, Martin Beauchamp. You only found out when I asked you to ring your brother and tell him what had happened," Laura laughed. She had been briefed on how Polly had come to be injured so was now fully aware of the situation.

Polly smiled at their play acting and found herself almost in tears again. This time though they were tears of happiness. They finished their tea and Polly started to drift off to sleep so they left her to rest. Laura went down to the kitchen to rescue Mrs Garside from Emma's attentions and take her home. Eric popped in now and again to see if she was awake, but when he left for the evening she was still asleep.

When she awoke the next morning she felt much better and tried to get out of bed to visit the bathroom. She put her feet to the ground and tried to stand up but her legs felt weak and the room began to spin. Just then Christopher walked in and rushed to her side.

"What do you think you're doing, Polly? Call for a nurse if you want to get up." He settled her back on the bed and went outside to the corridor where he managed to get a nurse to come and help Polly to the bathroom. When she returned, he settled her back under the covers and held her hand. He wasn't sure what to say as there was so much going on in his head.

"I'm sorry I snapped Polly, I was just frightened you were going to fall and hurt yourself all over again."

She smiled into his eyes, thinking how handsome he looked in his Air Force blue uniform. His hair was flopping into his eyes again and she wanted to brush it aside. "That's alright, Chris. I know you are worried, but I'm going to be alright, I promise."

"You'd better because I've written to mother and father and they are delighted that we are to be married. In fact, mother is coming back for the wedding, so you had better get better soon."

She closed her eyes and felt another wave of tears pressing against her eyelids. When she could hold them no more, they spilled down her cheeks and her mouth trembled with the effort of keeping them in. Chris was moved to tears himself as he watched her and climbed onto the bed to try and hold her, but she winced in pain as he touched her shoulder so he returned to the chair and held her hand. He felt totally frustrated at his inability to help her.

When she had recovered herself a little, he kissed her good hand which he held tightly between his own. "I don't know what to say, Polly. I just wish I could make you better."

"I know, Chris. It's just that I lost a lot of blood and I feel quite weepy all the time. I'm sure it's because I'm weak at the moment."

He stood up suddenly and dashed out of the room. She thought she had hurt his feelings in some way, but he came bounding back in no time.

"Now that everyone knows we are engaged, I thought it was time you had an engagement ring. I hope you like this, Polly. It belonged to my grandmother and mum said you should have it."

He opened a deep red leather ring box and took out the most beautiful ruby and diamond ring she had ever seen. She offered her left hand and he slid the ring onto her third finger. It was a perfect fit.

"Chris, this is absolutely the best ring you could have given me."

"I can't wait to marry you, Polly. What about the spring, shall we say April next year, my darling?"

"April sounds lovely to me," she answered and leaned forward into his embrace. It was a little awkward considering her wounded shoulder but it just felt nice to be close to him again.

Suddenly she had a thought, "When did you write to your parents? I thought we decided to keep it to ourselves for a while."

He looked a little sheepish, "I wrote just after Emma was born and mum replied almost straight away. You needn't have been worried about them, Polly. I know dad was a bit funny about everything and wanted me to marry somebody with connections, but he realises how topsy turvy everything is now and thinks we should grab what happiness we can."

"Will you tell Lady Beauchamp that I love the ring, and thank her for me for letting me have it."

"Yes, I'll write tonight. She doesn't know about your brush with death yet so I'll have to fill her in on that too. Father is very proud of you though."

"How does he know?"

"Martin told him after you were brought back here. He sends his love and best wishes for a speedy recovery."

"Chris – what happened to Jane and the German pilot?" she asked quietly.

"I think Martin would be better telling you that than me. He was there so he can fill you in on the details."

"Alright, I'll ask him when I see him next."

"What I do know though, is that Laura let them have the spare key to your house on Beck Hill and they have found a radio transmitter hidden under the floor of a wardrobe."

"Really? Well, I never thought our little house would become so notorious," she giggled in amazement.

There was a knock on the door and the nurse brought in breakfast for Polly, who was feeling much better and couldn't wait to tuck into her food.

Chris left her to go and eat his in the kitchen with Mrs Garside and when he returned, she was fast asleep again.

Her road to recovery was swift, thanks to her youth and the love and care of the staff at the hospital. When she was able to go home, Laura made it her mission in life to get her fully better in time for her wedding the following April.

The bullet hadn't penetrated too deeply but had been deflected off her shoulder bone and travelled up and out the top. The muscle was badly torn of course, but it could have been so much worse.

Martin had not had the time to speak to her about her adventure before her release from the hospital as he had mopping up duties to see to. He hoped she was sufficiently strong enough to hear what had happened.

He called round to the house in Chapel Lane a couple of days after her discharge from hospital. The window of the sitting room where she was resting looked directly onto the street at the front and she saw through the net curtains, a khaki clad individual approaching through the drizzling rain, the summer sun long gone and lost to a wet November. Laura let him in through the front door and he walked down the short corridor and tapped on the living room door.

"Come in, Martin," she said cheerily.

He entered the room and seemed to fill it with his bulk. He leaned forward and kissed her on her cheek before sitting opposite her next to the fire.

146

"It's good to see you looking so well, Polly," he began.

"It's very nice to see you again, too," she replied, thinking to herself that she would never have believed she would say those words to Martin Beauchamp of all people.

"I've never had the chance to speak to you since that day." He didn't need to say which day as it was engrained in her mind.

"I know you've had a lot to do, so don't worry about it."

Laura walked in with tea at that moment and Polly asked her to stay so she sat on the sofa. Emma was sleeping peacefully in her cot upstairs.

"I thought I'd better come round and let you know what has happened since we last spoke properly."

They waited for him to continue.

"I hope it doesn't upset you, Polly," he began tentatively.

"Don't worry, Martin. I'm a lot stronger than I was. Take your time. I'm interested to know what has happened since I blacked out on the stretcher."

He smiled, "Yes, it's a good job you're not heavy, Polly. Those poor stretcher bearers really struggled up that slope."

She laughed, "I know, I was dreading having to walk back up."

The tension eased a little as he began to tell her how he had gone for help to Parker's farm where he had telephoned his HQ and told them what the situation was with Eric. "They said they would send some men to help us to get Eric out of there. I wasn't aware at that time that Jane and the German pilot had turned up and everything went haywire so I waited about half an hour giving the men time to get from base to Horkstow Road and then went back to wait for them. I just wish now that I hadn't waited so long and just come back to you. I feel so guilty about that, Polly."

"Well, you needn't, silly. If you had come back earlier you would have been caught out too."

"Yes, I know, but I shouldn't have left you in such danger."

"You did what you had to do, Martin. Now carry on with the story."

"Well, just as we reached the lip of the earth works we heard a gunshot and I heard you cry out. I ordered the men - there were six of us altogether, to make their way round the back of the copse and I went forward slowly, trying to keep to the cover of the gorse bushes on the banks. I found my way through the tangle of branches to the clearing and heard raised voices speaking German. I realised that you must have been discovered and immediately rushed forward. I thought I would play on the fact that Jane thought I hated you but was *her* friend. Thankfully, it worked. She let me approach but I saw you bleeding on the ground and thought she had killed you. The German pilot was threatening Eric, so while he was distracted I managed to get the gun out of Jane's hand. She was very strong, Polly. They must train them hard over there."

Polly laughed at his expression. "Go on, what happened next?"

"I had to struggle with her for a second or two before over-powering her and in the meantime the pilot saw what was happening and ran off. By this time the others had arrived and I handed her over to them. The medics gave me some water and you woke up at that point so you know the rest."

"But I heard a rifle shot, Martin. Was that the pilot?"

"Yes, he was shot trying to escape."

"Good riddance is what I say," Laura interjected, lightening the conversation slightly.

"What about Jane?" Polly wanted to know.

"She was taken to HQ and the army interrogated her but she was a tough girl and wouldn't say a word. In the end she was sent to the Tower of London where she was tried and executed as a spy." I had to attend the trial but it was done in secret so I couldn't let you know anything about it. No doubt it will come to light in the future, but for now it must remain top secret."

He looked over at Laura who made the sign of the cross on her body and promised never to breathe a word of anything she had heard. Polly laughed at her antics but Martin was sombre.

"I'm sorry, Laura but it is vital that no-one knows anything or my life could be in danger too."

This sobered both of them up. "Sorry, Martin, we won't say a word, honest."

He drained his tea cup and then got up to go. "Don't forget both of you. Be like Dad and keep Mum."

"We will, don't worry, but before you go, Martin, what about your hands? I thought you had been invalided out of the army because you couldn't fire a gun."

"That's what I wanted everyone to believe. I owe you a great deal, Polly. Your first aid treatment on the boat saved my fingers and they are almost as good as new again." He waved a gloved hand in front of her. "They aren't as bent and disfigured as I made out. It was

148

necessary to keep the illusion going so that Jane wouldn't suspect anything.

"Well you're very good at it, Martin, that's all I can say," Polly said earnestly and they all laughed.

Chapter 19

Christopher had been flying Wellington bombers from Elsham airfield for months. He was so tired he didn't know what day it was. Sometimes, he slept in his flying suit because he was so weary when he got back from a bombing raid he couldn't be bothered to take it off. His surroundings were basic but reasonably comfortable. Being a pilot officer he had a room to himself which went with the rank but his men were only yards away in a Nissen hut. The iron bedstead and thin mattress were adequate for what sleep he managed to get and he had a picture of Polly on his bedside table, which cheered him up every time he looked at it. The walls were decorated with maps, timetables, rotas and the trappings of leadership. The office he used for his administration duties was decorated in much the same style. He was never far away from his work. Since Pearl Harbour in December 1941, the Americans had arrived in number at the base. They already had a contingent of Canadian pilots so they flew multi-national personnel on operations over Germany. The ultimate control at bomber command was British and the system seemed to work very well. They flew in strict rotation with Spitfire escort joining them from Lincoln to fight off any enemy fighters they may encounter on the way.

It was a few weeks before their wedding and he was due to go on a raid that evening but was finishing a letter to Polly when he heard somebody shouting. He went outside to see what was going on and saw one of the flight sergeants running from the control room shouting to the fire crews to be on standby. Christopher's opposite number had been sent on a secret mission over enemy territory but no-one knew anything about it, apart from the crew involved, and they would open their orders once on the plane. He looked up as he heard the tell-tale drone of a Wellington bomber coming in from the east. He could tell it was limping in to land by its erratic movement and noticed that the landing gear wasn't down.

Just then someone shouted and pointed to a Spitfire which was coming in faster but just as erratic as the first. Christopher ran to the control room to see what was going on as two planes landing in such close proximity was a recipe for disaster.

"What's going on?" he shouted trying to make himself heard over the din inside the small room.

"Two planes, sir. Both of them have been shot up quite badly and neither have any communications equipment working and no radar. "We're trying to signal to the Spit to land immediately, but they haven't seen the Wellington coming in above. If the Wellington tries to land too soon, it will flatten the Spit, sir."

Christopher ran outside just in time to see the Spitfire lower its landing gear but it was too late, the Wellington was oblivious to the smaller plane and came down directly on top of it. The resulting blast knocked Christopher off his feet, but like the others, he immediately got up and jumped on a fire engine as it raced to the scene. No-one survived the ball of flame but Christopher battled alongside the fire crew to extinguish the flames and when they had finished all that was left was a pile of twisted and charred metal.

The ground crew pulled out the bodies of both crews from the planes. The ambulance took them away leaving morale at an all time low. Christopher's crew had to put it behind them that evening and complete their mission as ordered but everyone was glad to land safely back at Elsham after a successful operation. It was Pilot Officer Beauchamp's job to write to the families of the dead British crew to inform them of the tragic loss of life.

A week later he and five others formed a guard of honour and fired a volley of shots over the graves of the airmen who had died on that tragic day.

When he arrived back at the base his Wing Commander called him into the office and asked him to sit down.

"We've had a bit of a miserable time of it lately, Chris. Haven't we?"

"Yes, sir, you could say that, but it would be a bit of an understatement."

"Three planes down on one mission, doesn't bode well does it? We need more pilots, Chris, and we need them quickly. Any ideas?"

"Poor blighters," Chris remarked referring to the crews of the three planes shot down over Germany the previous day. "No, sir, I'm all out of ideas."

"I've got a proposition for you," the Wing Commander reached into his desk draw and withdrew a bottle of Jack Daniels, a gift from the American Air Force contingent, and poured a generous amount into two tumblers, giving one to Chris. "Cheers."

"Cheers, sir. What's this proposition?"

"You've flown forty or more missions in Wellington bombers and countless hours in Spitfires. I want you to stand down for a few months and help train the next batch of would-be pilots."

Christopher was stunned and his glass of whisky stopped in mid-movement before he carried on and took a large gulp.

"I don't know what to say, sir."

"When I used the word 'proposition' I really meant order, Chris. You're tired and we need good men like you to train others to be just as good, if not better. What do you say?"

"I'm getting married in two weeks, sir. Where are you thinking of sending me?"

"That's the bug bear I'm afraid. You're going to Canada to take over a pilot training school near Toronto. You'll be away for some time. Of course, you can take your bride with you if she'll go, but I know what these local girls are like, most of them have never been out of the village."

Chris thought of Polly, and the fact that she did indeed fit the description to a tee; the only exception being that she had been over on the ferry to Hull occasionally when she was younger, not forgetting the trip to Dunkirk of course.

"I'll just have to persuade her, won't I, sir?"

"That's the ticket. Off you go, you've got a forty eight hour pass. I know it's not long but you've got a lot of fast talking to do." He added as an aside, "Doesn't your mother live in Canada at the moment?"

"Step–mother, sir," he corrected. "She does indeed in fact she's living near Toronto with her sister."

"Perfect, she can help persuade your fiancée to stretch her wings a bit. Pardon the pun," he smiled.

Christopher drained his glass and saluted as he left the room. He had no idea what he was going to tell Polly or whether or not she would go with him to Canada. Asking around he found there were no vehicles to take him to Barton so he used one of the camp bicycles and rode over to Barton as fast as he could.

He caught up with Polly as she was walking home that evening. Thanks to the double daylight hours it would be ages before it got dark. He caught up with her at the corner of Holydyke and Brigg Road, near the Wheatsheaf pub, bringing the bike to a rapid stop by her side making her jump. She laughed and was delighted to see him.

"Hello, Chris. This is a lovely surprise. What are you doing here?"

"I've got a forty eight hour pass, Polly. I need to talk to you about something."

He looked serious and her heart did a triple somersault as she thought of all the awful things that might have happened.

"Are you alright?" she stopped and looked into his eyes trying to read him.

"Yes, I'm fine." He wanted to discuss things with her once they were back at Laura's house so he played for time.

"Are we still getting married?" she asked quietly.

"Of course we are, silly. Look, let's get back to Laura's and I'll tell you all about it."

Polly was relieved and smiled again, taking comfort from his arm around her shoulders as they walked, with him pushing the bike along. Unfortunately, things weren't going to be that easy, as they found out when they walked through the back door. They had the shock of their lives when George came through from the living room with an empty cup and saucer in his hands.

"George!" Polly squealed and threw herself at him covering his face with kisses. Chris rescued the cup and saucer from George before he dropped it amid the onslaught of questions and hugs.

"I think I'll come back more often if this is the welcome I get," George said drily, as he tried to control Polly's enthusiasm. Laura stood at the door and watched with tears of laughter in her eyes.

Once they had settled down, it was impossible for Chris to say what he had come to say as George hadn't been home for well over a year so he was the centre of attention. Little Emma had been introduced to her father and they had become friends, so she sat importantly on her daddy's knee playing with his braces. After catching up with the news from everywhere George gave them an account of the fighting in North Africa and then followed up with his transfer to Italy. He had been fighting there for some months and had earned some leave. He was home for a month and then had to rejoin his unit. He would be at home for the wedding and Polly was overjoyed.

"You know what this means, don't you George?" she asked.

"What's that?" he replied

"You can give me away. Please say you will, it would really make the day special for us all to be together again on my wedding day."

"Well, what an honour. Of course I'll give you away, Polly. Thanks for asking me."

Laura stood up and took Emma off George's lap and went to change her nappy. George stood up too and reached for his uniform jacket.

"We're going to see my mum and dad now. They don't know I'm here yet so it's going to surprise them no end."

"I bet your mam will cry, George. She'll be so pleased to see you."

"Women! They're always crying – if they're happy they cry and if they're miserable they cry. You can't win."

Laura brought Emma back into the room who grinned toothily, clapping her hands, very happy to have both her parents in one place at the same time.

After they had left Polly started to tidy the room but Chris caught her hand and made her sit down.

"I've got something really important to tell you, Polly. Keep still for a minute will you?"

She sat down and folded her hands on her lap waiting for him to speak. He was silent for a while searching for the right words to break the news of his transfer and dreaded her response if she wouldn't go with him.

"Well, go on then. I'm waiting," she said airily.

"I'm being posted ..... after the wedding of course. You can come too if you want to, please say you will."

Polly was in shock as she sat staring at him, a jumble of thoughts going through her head.

"Where to?" she asked bluntly.

"Canada," he answered shortly.

"Canada! They're not at war in Canada." The words exploded from her lips as she stood up and started pacing the room. "Canada!" she said again.

"I know its short notice, but I've only just found out myself. I've got a forty eight hour pass so that we can make plans." He looked keenly into her eyes trying to second guess what her answer would be.

"What will you do there?"

"I've been posted to a flying school near Toronto. I'm being stood down as I've flown so many missions without a break. I'll be gone for months, Polly. I couldn't bear it if you didn't come too."

"It's just such a shock, Chris. I expected we would be staying here. I've lived here all my life. Laura and Emma are here. I'll have to leave them."

"I know it's a lot to ask but we will be husband and wife and just think of the adventures we can have there. It's not forever, Polly. We'll come back after a few months."

She looked into his worried face and knew she couldn't let him down.

"Alright, Chris. I'll come with you."

"Oh, Polly," his voice was unsteady with relief as he took her hands. "I'm so happy. I seem to have been waiting a very long time for you, so to know you would do this for me is absolutely wonderful. I know you'll be sacrificing a great deal but I promise you we will be happy."

"I know, Chris. Believe me, I've waited just as long for you and nothing will come between us, absolutely nothing."

They shared a long kiss and settled down on the sofa for a cuddle together, making plans as they talked and shared their hopes and dreams for the future.

When Laura and George returned they told them of the posting abroad and Laura was surprised but knew a wife's place was with her husband. She offered a home for them when they came back for which they were grateful, but there were more pressing matters to discuss, like wedding preparations.

George and Chris took themselves off to the Coach and Horses public house for a pint while the women talked endlessly about weddings and babies. Wedding dress material was as rare as gold dust so Polly had bought a nice lemon and white costume and a tiny lemon hat with a feather sweeping around the side. Her shoes were white and she was to carry a small posy of lemon tulips and daffodils as there was nothing else available at that time of the year. Laura thought she would look stunning and said so.

When the men returned a couple of hours later, Emma was asleep in her cot and Polly and Laura were writing lists of what she ought to take with her. Chris had no idea what her wedding outfit was going to be like of course and he was happy that he would be in his dress uniform which meant he didn't have to think about it.

*****

The week of the wedding arrived and Polly didn't know if she was happy or sad. When she thought about leaving Laura and Emma she felt like changing her mind, but when she thought of life without

Chris, she found the pain unbearable. She knew in her heart of hearts that she had found her soul mate.

She had given in her notice at work so her goodbyes had been said to everyone. She would see them on her wedding day of course, but they knew she would be away for some months so, of course, there had been tears, especially from Mrs Garside. Eric was going to take over her position as she had trained him so well. He too was sorry to see her go but would always be grateful to her and Martin for coming to his rescue that day. He felt that they had saved his life as he had no doubts Jane and her friend had come back to finish him off.

She was wandering around the house feeling a little lost without a job to go to when there was a knock on the door. George went to answer it and she could voices in the hallway outside the living room. The door opened and she had the shock of her life when in walked Lady Beauchamp. She was carrying a large, unwieldy cardboard box and Polly nearly jumped out of her skin when it was placed in her hands with a huge smile from Lady Beauchamp.

"What's this? What's going on? I'm sorry madam, but it's just such a shock to see you." she stuttered trying to stop herself from tearing open the box.

"Open it and see, Polly. I hope you like it."

Polly put the box on the sofa and started to undo the string. Laura and George were stood back watching. "Hurry up Polly, I can't wait to see what it is," said Laura impatiently.

As the lid of the box came off and the layers of tissue were parted, a beautiful oyster satin wedding dress was revealed.

"But, this is lovely. Is it for me?" she asked with tears in her eyes.

"Of course it's for you, my dear. It's a present from my husband and myself. We hope you like it. I understand that wedding dresses are in short supply over here at the moment, but there's no shortage in Canada."

Polly picked the dress up and carried it to the window to admire the neat stitching, the embroidery and the seed pearls sewn onto the bodice.

"It's absolutely beautiful, madam. Thank you so much. I really don't know what to say. Is it really mine?"

"Yes, it's really yours, and you will be the most beautiful bride ever wearing this on Saturday."

"You can wear the outfit you bought for going away in, Polly. You'll look lovely," Laura suggested.

And so she did. Polly married her handsome sweetheart on a perfect April Saturday. All their friends were around them making the day the happiest she had ever known. The future beckoned the happy couple and they took their first steps together out of St Mary's church, her gaze encompassing them as they all smiled and laughed together, congratulations echoing in their ears.

THE END